Triple Trouble
with
Jeremy James

David Henry Wilson was born in London in 1937 and educated at Dulwich College and Pembroke College, Cambridge. Before retirement, he lectured at the universities of Bristol and Konstanz, Germany, where he founded the student theatre. His plays have been widely performed in England, America, Germany and Scandinavia, and his children's books – especially the Jeremy James series – have been translated into several languages. His novel *The Coachman Rat* has been acclaimed in England, America and Germany. He is married with three grown-up children and lives in Taunton, Somerset.

Triple Trouble with Jeremy James

David Henry Wilson

Illustrated by Axel Scheffler

MACMILLAN CHILDREN'S BOOKS

Elephants Don't Sit on Cars first published 1977 by Chatto & Windus Ltd
Never Say Moo to a Bull first published 1979 under the title
Getting Rich with Jeremy James by Chatto & Windus Ltd,
published 1990 by Pan Books Ltd
How the Lion Lost His Lunch first published 1980 under the title
Beside the Sea with Jeremy James by Chatto & Windus Ltd

This edition published 2006 by Macmillan Children's Books
a division of Macmillan Publishers Limited
20 New Wharf Road, London N1 9RR
Basingstoke and Oxford
www.panmacmillan.com

Associated companies throughout the world

ISBN-13: 978-0330-44101-8
ISBN-10: 0-330-44101-9

Text copyright © David Henry Wilson 1977, 1979, 1980, 1996
Illustrations copyright © Axel Scheffler 1996

1 3 5 7 9 8 6 4 2

A CIP catalogue record for this book is available from
the British Library.

Typeset by Intype Libra Ltd
Printed and bound in Great Britain by Mackays of Chatham plc, Kent

Elephants Don't Sit on Cars

For
Chris,
Jenny,
and (of course) J.J.

Contents

CHAPTER ONE

The Elephant on Daddy's Car

'Mummy,' said Jeremy James, 'there's an elephant sitting on Daddy's car.'

'Yes, dear,' said Mummy, eyes fixed on hands fixed on dough fixed on table.

'Mummy, why is the elephant sitting on Daddy's car?'

'I expect it's tired, dear. It'll probably get up and go away soon.'

'Well, it hasn't,' said Jeremy James two minutes later. 'It hasn't got up. The car's gone down, but the elephant hasn't got up. Mummy, do you think I ought to tell Daddy?'

'No, no, leave your father,' said Mummy, 'you know he hates being interrupted when he's working.'

'Daddy's watching a football match on television.'

'If Daddy says he's working, he's working.'

'Well, there's an elephant sitting on his car,' said Jeremy James.

Mummy thumbed sultanas into the dough to make eyes and noses.

'And the car doesn't look very happy about it,' said Jeremy James.

'Jeremy James,' said Mummy. 'Elephants don't sit on cars.'

'Well this one does.'

'Elephants don't sit on cars. If Mummy says elephants don't sit on cars, dear, then elephants don't sit on cars.'

'But—'

'They don't. Finish! Now play with your train set.'

Jeremy James sat on the carpet, and played with his train set, and thought about the elephant on Daddy's car, and thought about how stubborn Mummies can be when they want to be, and how if he was a Mummy and his son said there was an elephant on Daddy's car, he would say 'What a clever boy,' and 'Thank you for telling me,' and 'Here's some money for an ice cream.' Instead of just 'Elephants don't sit on cars.'

'Goal!' said the television set in the sitting room.

'Goal!' said Daddy, hard at work.

And the elephant was still sitting on Daddy's car.

'Mummy,' said Jeremy James, for the latest development couldn't be ignored. 'Mummy, the elephant has just done its Number Two all over Daddy's car.'

But Mummy's face merely twitched like a fly-flicking elephant's ear, and she said nothing.

'Gosh, and *what* a Number Two! Mummy, you should see the elephant's Number Two! Mummy, why do elephants do such big Number Twos? I can't do a Number Two like that! Mine isn't even a thousandth as big as that! *What* a Number Two!'

'Jeremy James, if you go on talking like that, I shall send you straight to bed. Now play with your train set and let's have no more elephant talk, and certainly no more about Number Twos. Do you hear?'

'Yes, Mummy.'

No Number Twos. Anyone would think that Number Twos were unhealthy. Only look what happened when you didn't do a Number Two. Then it was: 'Jeremy James, have you done your Number Two? You haven't done your Number Two? Then sit there until you have.' Now tell them an elephant's done his Number Two on Daddy's car, and suddenly it's rude. Why can't grown-ups make up their minds?

Jeremy James played with his train set.

Jeremy James looked out of the window. The elephant was gone.

'Mummy,' said Jeremy James.

'What is it now?' said Mummy, half in and half out of the oven.

'The elephant's gone.'

'Hmmph.'

That was a typical grown-up word: 'Hmmph.' It was for grown-ups only, and meant whatever they wanted it to mean. Jeremy James had tried to use a 'Hmmph' once himself. Mummy had said, 'Have you done your Number Two?' (at one of those times when Number Two wasn't rude) and he'd replied 'Hmmph', because that was how grown-ups got out of awkward questions like, 'Will you buy me something nice today,' or, 'Why can't I have a toy racing car like

Timothy's?' Only Jeremy James obviously didn't know how to use it, because Mummy told him to speak properly, even though he'd said 'Hmmph' perfectly properly.

Daddy came out of the sitting room, with his face as long as an elephant's nose.

'They lost,' said Daddy. 'Right at the end. An own goal.'

Then Daddy leaned on the kitchen doorpost as he always did when he'd been working (and sometimes when he *was* working), and watched Mummy working, presumably to make sure she was doing everything right. Jeremy James had tried leaning on the doorpost once and saying, as Daddy always ended up by saying, 'Will it be long, dear?' But instead of getting Mummy's normal 'Hmmph', he'd had a 'Now don't you start!' and been sent off to play with his train set, which he was sick of anyway.

'Will it be long, dear?' said Daddy.

'Hmmph,' said Mummy.

'Now don't you start,' said Jeremy James quietly.

'An own goal,' said Daddy. 'Right at the end.'

'Was that goal Number Two?' asked Jeremy James.

'I don't know what's got into that child,' said Mummy. Daddy elbowed himself upright off the doorpost, took one hand out of one pocket ('Take your hands out of your pockets, Jeremy James!') yawned, and announced, 'Maybe I'll go and clean the car.'

Mummy didn't say, 'There won't be time before

tea,' though Daddy waited quite a while for her to say it, and so Daddy eventually left the kitchen, crossed the dining room, entered the hall, opened the front door, and went out of the house.

Jeremy James stood at the window and wondered what new words Daddy would use.

Daddy didn't use any words. Daddy's mouth fell open, and then Daddy came back to the house, opened the front door, entered the hall, crossed the dining room, and held himself up by the kitchen doorpost.

'The car!' said Daddy. Then his mouth opened and shut several times as if he'd just been pulled out of the water. 'The car!' he said again.

'What's the matter with it?' asked Mummy, spreading hand-cream over the bread.

'It's been ruined. It . . . it . . . it's ruined! It looks as if it's been completely squashed! Completely and utterly squashed!'

'Oh John,' said Mummy, who only called Daddy John when she was very upset or when she wanted some money, 'Oh John, there . . . there isn't . . . um . . . sort of . . . dung all over it as well, is there?'

'Yes,' said Daddy, 'there jolly well is! I've never seen anything like it, either. Must have been a herd of cows dancing on the thing!'

'It wasn't a herd of cows,' said Jeremy James, 'it was an elephant. And I saw it. And I told Mummy, but she wouldn't listen.'

'An elephant!' said Daddy. 'You saw an elephant on the car?'

'Yes,' said Jeremy James, 'and I saw it do its Number Two as well.'

'Then why the . . . . didn't one of you tell me?'

'Hmmph!' said Mummy, and Jeremy James played with his train set.

CHAPTER TWO

Shopping

'I'm going shopping,' said Mummy. 'Do you want to come with me?'

'Will you buy me something nice?' asked Jeremy James.

'You can't expect me to buy you something nice every time I go shopping,' said Mummy. 'I don't go shopping just to buy you something nice, and in any case it's the end of the month, so I can't afford it.'

'Are you going to buy cornflakes?' asked Jeremy James.

'Yes,' said Mummy.

'Well I'd sooner go without my cornflakes, and have something nice instead,' said Jeremy James.

'Hmmph,' said Mummy. 'Get your coat on.'

'I'm quite warm, though, Mummy.'

'Get your coat on.'

That, thought Jeremy James, is typical. Just because *she's* cold, *I* have to put a coat on.

Jeremy James and Mummy went to the shops. They walked. Jeremy James would much rather have gone by bus, but Mummy said they would come back by bus when they had the shopping to carry. It was healthier to walk. It was also cheaper to walk. So Jeremy James pretended he was a bus, and steered in and out of people till he almost steered straight into an old lady, and then Mummy told him to walk properly, so he became a guardsman instead.

The trouble with Mummy when she went shopping was that she liked all the wrong shops. Boring clothes shops and china shops and food shops especially. She only bought things in the food shops, but she spent hours in the clothes shops touching things, and hours outside the china shops gazing in as if it were the zoo. Even in the food shops she spent hours touching and gazing. She fingered every packet of cheese, opened every box of eggs, weighed every piece of meat. The only thing she didn't spend hours on was tins of fruit, and tins of fruit were the one thing Jeremy James did like looking at. Apart from boxes of sweets and bars of chocolate and packets of cake. And Mummy didn't spend any time on them either. Mummy didn't really seem to have much idea about shopping.

Next to the food supermarket was a toy shop. Its windows were full of games and soldiers and tanks and guns and footballers and bows and arrows, and a few silly things for girls. Jeremy James noted all this as they walked past the toy shop, and he pointed it out to Mummy. He said, 'Oh look, Mummy, look at all the games and soldiers and tanks and guns and footballers and bows and arrows, and those silly things for girls.' Mummy said, 'Hmmph,' and wouldn't stop because they would be late for dinner,

or something. Jeremy James followed her with his feet, leaving his eyes behind, and bumped into a fat woman with a fur coat and a poodle. The fat woman with the fur coat and the poodle said something a bit like 'Hmmph!' but with rather more 'ph' than 'hmm', and Jeremy James said 'Ouch' and ran after Mummy, while the fat woman looked angry and moved her lips as if she was talking.

Mummy started picking up chickens. They were frozen chickens in paper wrappings, and they all looked alike, but Mummy studied them very carefully, one after another. Jeremy James fixed his eye on one particular chicken Mummy had just put down, and there was no doubt whatsoever that she picked the same one up again a minute later.

'You've seen that one already,' said Jeremy James. 'I know, 'cos I've been watching it.'

Mummy didn't seem to hear.

'Mummy, won't we be late for dinner, or something?' said Jeremy James.

But examining chickens seemed really to make Mummy rather hard of hearing. Jeremy James wandered off to the tinned fruit department. He looked up at the coloured walls of mouth-watering pictures: pineapples, pears, peaches, cherries, raspberries, strawberries, and mandarin oranges – sweet mandarin oranges – all in their own juice which was deliciously cold after you'd put the tin in the fridge for a while. The only trouble with tinned fruit was that you always wanted a second helping, and Mummy always said 'No' because there was nothing left. They should make the tins a bit bigger so you could have a second helping. When he was grown up, of course, Jeremy James would buy *two* tins, just to make sure, but he'd suggested that to Mummy and she'd said something about tinned fruit not growing on trees, and that apparently meant no.

In front of the wall of juicy pictures were big wire thingamabobs all full of tins just like the tins up against the wall. People took tins from the thingamabobs and put them in their trolleys, leaving the others standing intact. This seemed odd to Jeremy James, because although the tins were all the same, the tins up against the wall *looked* nicer. They were sort of regular and more juicy-looking. Grown-ups probably don't notice these things, because when they're taking

15

tins of fruit they're in a hurry and simply go for the nearest one, which is always in the wire thingamabob. The same with cakes and bars of chocolate – they just take whatever's nearest because they're not interested in interesting things. They only pick and choose when it's boring things like meat or cheese or chickens.

The more Jeremy James studied the wall of tins, the more obvious it became that those were the *best* tins. That was why the people who owned the shop put them further away – they were probably saving them for themselves when the shop closed. After all, when Mummy bought fresh pears, peaches, oranges, apples and so on, some were always nicer than others, and she always insisted they should eat the nasty ones first. That must be the way grown-ups did things. Nasties first. It was the same with dinner and dessert. She never let him have dessert till he'd finished dinner. And he had to have his bath before he could have his bed-time story. And he had to tidy his room before he got his piece of chocolate. Nasties first, that was the rule. And so the best tins of fruit were those against the wall, and the best tin of all must be the one most difficult to get at – the last tin that anybody could reach. It must be that tin there (he was in front of the mandarin orange department) – the tin in the middle of the bottom row.

Jeremy James imagined saying to Mummy, 'Mummy, this is the best tin of mandarin oranges in the whole shop.' And Mummy would say he was a clever boy, and she might buy him an ice cream even though it was the end of the month. In fact she might make it his regular job – choosing the best tin of fruit every time they went shopping. Jeremy James smiled to himself. Life is simple when you use your brain. Jeremy James looked round quickly to make sure the shop people weren't looking, because you could be quite certain they would try to stop him taking the best tin of mandarin oranges in the whole shop. No one was looking. Jeremy James eased past the wire thingamabob. Jeremy James bent down. Jeremy James put his hand round the best tin of mandarin oranges in the whole shop. Jeremy James pulled. The best tin of mandarin oranges didn't move. Of course it didn't move – there were two more tins resting on it holding it down. And so with his left hand Jeremy James pushed the two holding-down tins, and with his right hand he pulled out the best tin of mandarin oranges.

And then a strange and terrible thing happened. The wall of tins seemed to do a kind of knees-bend. And then the tins started falling down. First of all they fell from round the best tin which wasn't there any more, and then they fell all over the place. Some of them fell on Jeremy James, but he quickly jumped out of the way, and stood behind the wire thingama-bob, watching. Tins were bouncing and rolling every-where, and it wasn't just mandarin oranges – peaches, pears and pineapples joined in as well. And the people in the shop all stopped moving around and turned to look in the direction of the tins of fruit, and two or three shop people came hurrying along with pale faces

and frowning eyebrows, and an old lady pointed at her foot and limped away muttering, and a baby cried, and more tins fell and rolled, and a very big shop man in a grey suit started giving orders and making the other people in the shop run around, and there were veins standing out in his forehead, and his eyes were bulgy, and he didn't look a very nice man, and his bulgy eyes settled on Jeremy James, and Jeremy James decided he'd better go back to Mummy. He was rather glad, when he turned round, that Mummy was already there.

'Come on, Jeremy James,' said Mummy. 'We'll be late for dinner.' Or something. Mummy took the best tin of mandarin oranges in the whole shop out of Jeremy James's hand, and slipped it into her trolley, and pulled Jeremy James along – rather roughly, he thought – to the cash desk.

As they left the shop, Jeremy James looked back. The shop people were still picking up tins, and the man in the grey suit still didn't look very nice. But Jeremy James knew why the man in the grey suit was angry. He'd wanted that tin of mandarin oranges for himself, that was why.

CHAPTER THREE

The Football Match

Every so often Daddy stopped working. That is to say, every so often Daddy admitted he had stopped working. Of course, he wasn't working when he was in bed, in the bath, in the kitchen, in the armchair, leaning on the doorpost, or watching television, but otherwise generally he *was* working. His study door was firmly closed, and from the study would come that profound stillness and silence of the man at work. You could sometimes hear a typewriter, too, but Daddy always said it was the bits in between the typewriter that were the real work, and the quieter he was, the harder he was working. That was what Daddy said.

But every so often, Daddy stopped working. And on Saturday afternoons he almost never worked. And on this particular Saturday afternoon, as on every other Saturday afternoon, he announced after lunch that he was going to take the afternoon off. There was, he had been led to believe, a football match on this afternoon, and as he felt in need of some fresh air, he might pop along to see it.

'Why don't you take Jeremy James?' said Mummy.

Daddy thought hard for a minute or two, wondering why he couldn't take Jeremy James, but it soon became clear from his silence that he couldn't find any particular reason. And so Jeremy James was wrapped up in his thickest sweater and his heaviest coat and his ear-warmingest ear-warmers, and went off hand-in-hand with Daddy, blowing clouds of dragon-breath over the winter landscape.

They didn't take the car because, said Daddy, it would be quicker to walk. Lots of cars went past them, soon leaving them far behind, but when Jeremy James pointed out that the cars were quicker than they were, Daddy simply murmured, 'You'll see', so Jeremy James and he went on walking. When they got near the football stadium, the pavement began to get more and more crowded, and very soon they were walking in the road, and Daddy was quite right, because they then started passing cars which hooted angrily. Jeremy James wanted to let go of Daddy's hand so that he could be a racing car zooming in and out of the leg-jungle, but Daddy made him hold tight; otherwise, as Daddy said, 'They'll turn you into a half-time message.'

Outside the ground itself, there were queues which were certainly the biggest queues in the world. The queues in Mummy's food shops weren't even queues compared with these queues. These were monster queues, with hundreds of thousands of people – most of them men, which made them even more different from the food-shop queues. A lot of the men looked very happy, and had bright scarves (mainly blue and

white) round their necks, with big flowers (also blue
and white) stuck in their coats. One or two men had
rattles (also blue and white) which were a lot bigger
than Jeremy James's old baby rattles that he had
grown out of long ago. These rattles were so big you
could never grow out of them, and they made a much
louder noise than a thousand of Jeremy James's old
baby rattles.

The queues moved a lot quicker than the food-
shop queues, and each time someone went into the
football ground, there was a clickety-click, which
turned out to be an iron bar you had to push through.
When Jeremy James pushed through, it went clickety-
click, just as it had done for the man in front of him,
but really when you thought about it, there didn't

seem much point, because you could have got into the ground much easier without the iron bar.

'I think we'll go in the stand,' said Daddy, 'it'll be more comfortable.' And so they joined another queue, which was much smaller than the first queue, and soon they were climbing up some steep steps, at the top of which was a man with a moustache and a red face who took Daddy's ticket. And then for the first time Jeremy James saw the football pitch. It was quite different to football pitches on the television, because this one was very big and grassy. You certainly couldn't get this big grassy one on to the little television screen at home, and that was a fact.

'Come on, Jeremy James!' said Daddy, and pulled him along to a place where people had their feet. When Daddy and Jeremy James arrived, the people took their feet away, and Daddy sat down. Jeremy James sat down as well, though he thought it a bit funny to sit down where people normally put their feet. It was hard, too.

'We're better off in the stand,' said Daddy. 'You can see better, too.'

'Is this the stand, Daddy?' asked Jeremy James.

'Yes,' said Daddy.

'Well why are we sitting down, then?' asked Jeremy James.

'This is where you sit down,' said Daddy.

'Then why's it called the stand?' asked Jeremy James.

'That's an interesting question,' said Daddy, 'but I haven't come here to give a lesson on semantics.'

Mummy, of course, would have said 'Hmmph', but Daddy often used long words that didn't exist when he couldn't answer a question. Semantics was one of his favourite words, though Jeremy James knew it was only the name of a tabby cat three doors away.

Someone was saying something over the loudspeaker. It sounded like, 'Worple shob worple forby gambridge Number Two,' and Jeremy James assumed he was checking that the footballers had all done the necessary before the game started. Grown-ups had a thing about going to the lavatory before you did anything.

Then all of a sudden everybody shouted, and some men came running on to the field, kicking a ball. They were dressed in red and white, and most of the shouting wasn't very friendly. But when more men came running on to the field, kicking another ball, and all dressed in blue and white, even Daddy started shouting a funny sort of 'worp worp!' shout, as if he knew them.

'Are they your friends, Daddy?' asked Jeremy James.

'They're the home team,' said Daddy.

Jeremy James was quite sure he had never seen any of the men at home, but Daddy was shouting again, and it was best not to interrupt.

A man in black – 'Has his grandma died, Daddy?' asked Jeremy James – blew a whistle, almost as well as Jeremy James could blow *his* whistle, everybody shouted again, and the men started kicking the ball and running round the field. Jeremy James watched for a little while, and Daddy told him the names of some of the men in blue, though Jeremy James didn't know any of them, and couldn't remember any of the them once Daddy had told him. Daddy said the men were trying to kick the ball into the net at the end of the pitch, but Jeremy James never saw anybody trying to kick the ball into the net at all. Most of the time the ball wasn't anywhere near the net, and the men seemed to be trying to kick it in any other direction *but* the net. Sometimes the men didn't even kick the ball, but kicked each other, and then everybody shouted and the man in black blew his whistle and waved his arms. Once the ball came up into the sitting-down stand, very near to Daddy, and Jeremy James reckoned even he could kick the ball closer to the net.

Nobody scored a goal, and the man in black at last blew the whistle, and the players walked slowly off the pitch. Daddy then started talking to the man next to him, and Jeremy James heard him say, 'The ref needs his blooming eyes tested.' So Jeremy James turned to the man next to him – who had glasses and a funny chin – and said, 'The ref needs his blooming eyes tested.' The man with glasses and a funny chin seemed a little surprised, so Jeremy James added, 'That's what my Daddy says.'

After some loud music and a lot of talking, the players came out again, and the man in black blew his whistle, and the running and kicking went on as before. Jeremy James noticed that when a man in blue kicked the ball or a man in red, the crowd was happy, and when a man in red kicked the ball or a man in blue, they lost their tempers and shouted nasty things. But obviously Daddy had made a mistake about the ball going into the net, because nobody seemed even to try and kick it in. Until hours and hours had gone by, and the man in black was looking at his watch as if he was learning to tell the time. And then suddenly one of the men in red kicked the ball very hard, and it went straight into the net.

'Oh good!' shouted Jeremy James. 'He's got it in! He got it in the net, Daddy!'

And then all the people with blue and white scarves and blue and white flowers turned round and looked at Jeremy James, because in the silence his voice came out loud and clear, and Daddy's face went rather red, and he told Jeremy James to keep quiet. And the man in black blew his whistle for a long time, and the players stopped running altogether, and those in red jumped up and down waving their arms, whilst those in blue walked slowly away watching their own feet, and everybody stood up and shouted 'Boo!', as if they wanted to frighten the men on the pitch. And when they'd finished shouting 'Boo!', the people started to shuffle out of the sitting-down stand, and Daddy and Jeremy James shuffled with them, till they were back in the air again, and entering the leg-jungle out in the street, passing cars which were still hooting angrily – in fact doing everything in reverse from when they had come.

'Did you enjoy it, dear?' asked Mummy when they got home.

'Yes thank you,' said Jeremy James, 'it was funny.'

'Who won?' Mummy asked Daddy.

'Hmmph!' said Daddy, 'I must get on with my work,' and he went into his study and closed the door firmly behind him. And he was so quiet that he must have been working very hard indeed.

CHAPTER FOUR

Uncle Arthur

It was two o'clock in the morning when Uncle Arthur arrived through the window of Jeremy James's bedroom. There was not a sound anywhere in the house, street, town – with the exception of the rumbling, stuttering, pig-snort muttering known as Daddy's Snore to everyone except Daddy, who called it Mummy's Snore. Otherwise it was all very quiet indeed.

Jeremy James, of course, was fast asleep, and would certainly have remained fast asleep if Uncle Arthur hadn't fallen and sat on his head. Having someone sitting on his head was enough to wake even Jeremy James.

Jeremy James didn't know it was Uncle Arthur sitting on his head, because when you've been fast asleep and are woken by being sat on and find that it's pitch dark anyway – well, it's difficult to know who's who and what's what.

So Jeremy James merely sat up in bed (when Uncle Arthur, who at the time was just somebody or the other, had stood up again), and asked who it was. There was a low mumbling noise, which sounded a bit like 'Hmmph', and then complete silence, except for some rather heavy breathing.

'Are you a doggy?' asked Jeremy James.

The doggy didn't reply.

Jeremy James reached out and switched on the light – for he had a switch right by his bed, in case he felt like weeing in the night.

When he had blinked a few times, he found himself looking at a rather funny little man dressed in a thick sweater and carrying a large sack.

'Hello,' said Jeremy James.

'Hello,' said the funny little man with the sweater and the sack.

'Who are you?' asked Jeremy James.

'Um . . . guess!' said the little man.

'Well, I know Father Christmas carries a sack like that,' said Jeremy James, 'but . . . well, it's not Christmas, and anyway Father Christmas has a long white beard, and you haven't. And Father Christmas isn't bald, and he doesn't wear glasses either. So you're not Father Christmas.'

'No,' said the little man. 'I'm not.'

'And you're not the chimney sweep,' said Jeremy James.

'Oh!' said the little man, 'what makes you say that?'

'Well, for one thing you're not covered in black, and for another, we haven't got any fireplaces, and chimney sweeps have to have fireplaces to sweep up, like we had in our last house. And you don't smell. At least, not much.'

'No, I'm not the chimney sweep,' said the little man.

'Well who are you, then?'

'Ah!' said the little man, looking round the room. 'Ah!'

'R.? R. what?'

'I'm . . . um . . . I'm your Uncle Arthur,' said the little man. 'That's who I am. Your dear old Uncle Arthur.'

'Oh!' said Jeremy James. 'I didn't know I had an Uncle Arthur.'

'No, well, you have now,' said Uncle Arthur. 'But . . . er . . . I think perhaps I'd better slip out again, and come back another time – seeing that it's so late.'

'Oh no,' said Jeremy James, 'I'll tell Mummy and Daddy you're here. I don't think they know I've got an Uncle Arthur either.'

'No, no, I wouldn't do that, son, if I were you. Don't wake them up. I'll . . . I'll come back.'

'It's no trouble,' said Jeremy James, already out of bed, heading for the door, and seeing a pile of pocket money and ice cream such as all grateful uncles are obliged to provide for little boys who do them favours.

'Wait, wait!' said Uncle Arthur. 'Wait!'

Jeremy James waited.

'Look . . .' said Uncle Arthur, 'um . . . look . . . your Mummy and Daddy aren't expecting me, you see. They don't know I'm coming. And actually . . . well . . . I don't want them to know I'm here, you see. It's . . . er . . . a secret.'

'A secret?'

'Yes, a secret.'

'You mean like Mummy's new dress which I mustn't tell Daddy about?'

'That's right, yes, just like Mummy's new dress!'

'Good,' said Jeremy James. Mummy's secret was worth twenty pence, and uncles are always more generous than mothers. 'I like uncles,' said Jeremy James, 'because uncles always give me things, and Mummy gave me twenty pence not to tell Daddy about her new dress.'

'Ah,' said Uncle Arthur. 'Well, if you keep this little secret, Johnnie my lad—'

'My name's not Johnnie! I'm Jeremy James.'

'Of course, Jeremy James . . . now, if you keep this little secret, I'll give you fifty pence. How's that?'

It's wonderful, said Jeremy James to himself. What is it that makes uncles so much more understanding than mothers – and aunts, if it comes to that? They seem to have a better sense of justice. It would be a better world if all aunts and mothers turned into uncles – and that's a fact.

'All right,' said Jeremy James.

'Here,' said Uncle Arthur, reaching into his pocket, and the money was absolutely real, and absolutely right. A shining 50p piece.

'And now,' said Uncle Arthur, 'I'll have to be going. I've got a train to catch.'

'Aren't you coming back?' asked Jeremy James.

'Well, not for a while,' said Uncle Arthur. 'I'm a very busy man.'

'I hope you'll come back soon,' said Jeremy James. 'I like uncles.'

Uncle Arthur turned towards the window, which was wide open. Jeremy James walked to the window himself, and saw a ladder leaning on the wall outside.

'Oh, you don't need to go out of the window,' said Jeremy James. 'I know how to open the front door. Come on.'

'No, no,' said Uncle Arthur, 'I always use the window. It's . . . um . . . more fun.'

Jeremy James nodded, as if he agreed. After all, fifty pence is fifty pence.

'Shall I pass your bag out to you?' asked Jeremy James, feeling it was the least he could do.

'Oh, thanks very much, Johnnie.'

'Jeremy James.'

'Jeremy James.'

But the bag turned out to be rather heavy, so Uncle Arthur had to climb back in again after all to get it. And in climbing back in, he scraped his leg on the window sill and said a word Daddy had once used when he dropped a hammer on his toe.

'Mummy says that's a naughty word,' said Jeremy James.

But Uncle Arthur used the same word again, which confirmed what Jeremy James had already long suspected: Mummy didn't really know what words were naughty and what weren't.

Uncle Arthur grabbed his bag, and climbed out of the window again.

'Goodnight, Uncle Arthur!' shouted Jeremy James, when Uncle Arthur had reached the bottom of the ladder.

Uncle Arthur looked up sharply, as if he wasn't too pleased, whispered goodnight, and ran rather fast out into the darkness of the back garden, so that Jeremy James couldn't see him any more.

'Mummy,' said Jeremy James at breakfast next morning. 'When's Uncle Arthur going to come and see us again?'

'Uncle Arthur?' said Mummy. 'You haven't got an Uncle Arthur.'

'Yes I have,' said Jeremy James. 'You know, the bald one who carries a sack.'

'Eat your cornflakes,' said Mummy, 'and don't talk nonsense.'

'He's the one who always comes in through the window.'

'You haven't got an Uncle Arthur, Jeremy James. Now finish your cornflakes.'

Grown-ups really do live in a different world.

CHAPTER FIVE

Feeding an Elephant

It was one of those bright blue-sky birdsong days when Mummy suddenly remembered that fresh air was good for you and the family hadn't been out for days weeks and months.

'Let's go to the zoo,' she said. Jeremy James smiled.

'What, today?' said Daddy. Jeremy James frowned.

'Yes, today,' said Mummy. 'We could do with some fresh air, and anyway we haven't been out for days weeks months.'

'But it's Saturday,' said Daddy.

'I know,' said Mummy.

'Well . . . the place'll be crowded, and I mean . . .'

'I suppose there's a football match on the television,' said Mummy.

'Well, yes, as it happens there is, but . . .'

And so Mummy, Daddy, and Jeremy James went to the zoo. Jeremy James loved the zoo, and most of the time Mummy and Daddy behaved quite well when they went to the zoo, probably because they liked it too. The only trouble was, they all liked different things. Daddy would settle in front of the lions' cage and start talking about noble beasts in captivity, and they would have to drag him away or he'd stay there till sleeping-time. Mummy was fascinated by the birds with their bright feathers, and would start talking about colourful nature, patterns, grace, and then *she* had to be dragged away. But what annoyed Jeremy James most was that both Mummy and Daddy loved the monkeys, and whilst he and Mummy could drag Daddy away from the lions, and he and Daddy could drag Mummy away from the birds, he all on his own hadn't got a chance of dragging both Mummy and Daddy away from the monkeys.

Today, Mummy and Daddy were extra keen on the monkeys.

'Look at that!' shrieked Mummy, as an ugly creature with a sore bottom jumped on to a rubber tyre and grinned.

'They're a scream,' said Daddy.

But they weren't a scream at all. The fact was that they didn't do anything that Jeremy James couldn't do just as well, but when monkeys did it, Mummy and Daddy laughed and thought it was wonderful, and when Jeremy James did it, he simply got told off. Only that very morning he had done a magnificent leap from the sofa on to Daddy's armchair – not to mention braving the raging river a thousand feet below – and had merely been drily told not to jump on the furniture. Not a laugh, not a clap . . . just,

'Don't jump on the furniture.' And when he swung
from the apple tree, did they gaze at him with love
and admiration in their eyes? No. Either they didn't
watch him at all, or if they did, they simply shouted,
'Mind the apples, Jeremy James!' or, 'If you tear your
trousers, you'll see what you get!' And as for bananas,
that was the unfairest cheat of all. They *gave*
bananas to the monkeys, just to see how they peeled
them, and when the monkeys peeled their bananas,
Mummy and Daddy would grin at each other and
say how clever the monkeys were. But if Jeremy James
asked for a banana (which he could peel a hundred
times quicker than any old monkey), they'd say, 'Wait
till tea-time,' and that was that.

Mummy and Daddy had got stuck in front of the
monkeys. They would be there all day, and that was

a fact, and Jeremy James couldn't see the joke or the point. So Jeremy James waited till one of the monkeys was being particularly clever (beating his chest and showing his teeth, which was apparently a marvellous trick that had all the grown-ups roaring with laughter), and slipped away into the crowd and off in the direction of the elephant house. Elephants, after all, were the biggest animals, and they were easily the most interesting. Elephants could do things that Jeremy James couldn't do at all. Like squirting water over themselves, picking up buns with their noses, and squashing cars. Elephants were really talented – not like monkeys.

There were lots of people at the elephant house, which wasn't a house at all, but a great big sort of playground with rails round it and with a ditch on the other side of the rails. The elephants could just about reach the rail with their trunks, and sniff up the buns and things people were giving them. Daddy never let Jeremy James feed any animals, because he said there were notices everywhere with 'Don't Feed The Animals' on them – but Daddy was the only one who ever saw these notices, and it was obvious that even if there *were* notices, the animals couldn't have written them, so they were unfair. *Everyone* likes buns and sweets and biscuits and things, and the animals liked them too, so Daddy was probably being mean.

In his pocket, Jeremy James had two slices of bread. He'd smuggled them out of the house. They weren't ordinary bread. They were bread with currants in. The sort of bread elephants dream about. And he'd brought them just for the elephants, and although he'd have liked a bite or two himself – especially of a curranty bit – he could see the expression on the elephant's face already, and he knew the elephant knew the currant bread was for *him*. So Jeremy James didn't take a single bite – not even to taste it.

'Here!' said Jeremy James, and reached out both slices at once. And then the elephant made a very silly mistake. He *took* both slices (with a scrapy, creepy, snuffly whiff of Jeremy James's hand), but between hand and mouth, very foolishly, he forgot there were two. One he tossed into his mouth, and the other he let fall right on to the edge of the ditch.

'Hey!' said Jeremy James, 'don't forget the other one!'

But the elephant, who must have been a very stupid elephant, not only forgot it, but also ignored Jeremy James completely. He just turned his head away and looked around for someone else to feed him. And Jeremy James's second slice of currant bread lay all uneaten on the edge of the ditch.

'There, look!' shouted Jeremy James.

'On the edge of the ditch, look!' shouted Jeremy James.

'Opposite your foot!' shouted Jeremy James.

The elephant nearly trod on it, but still didn't see it. Jeremy James remembered one of Daddy's words:

'It's opposite your blooming foot!' he shouted, but the elephant didn't take any notice.

There was only one thing Jeremy James could do. After all, a slice of currant bread is a slice of currant bread, and you don't smuggle currant bread out of the house just to leave it lying on the edge of a ditch. 'You're a stupid elephant,' said Jeremy James, as he slipped between the railings. 'You're as stupid as those monkeys.'

Jeremy James reached the edge of the ditch, and a great shout went up from the crowd behind as he picked up the slice of currant bread. Then everything seemed to go very quiet indeed. So quiet that Jeremy James turned round to see what was wrong, but all the people were still there – they were just quiet, that was all.

'Here!' said Jeremy James, holding out the currant bread. 'Come on, you stupid elephant!'

The elephant slowly turned his head, at last spotted the currant bread, and scrapy-creepy-snuffle-whiffed it out of Jeremy James's hand.

'And about time too!' said Jeremy James. Then he turned round, and squeezed back through the railings, straight into the grip of a man wearing a zoo-keeper uniform, a moustache, and a red face.

'Where's your mother and father?' said the moustache.

'I expect they're still wasting their time watching those monkeys,' said Jeremy James.

But just at that moment Mummy and Daddy arrived, and their faces looked rather red too, and when they saw Jeremy James they both said at the same time, 'Where have you been?' And then the moustache said something to them, and then Daddy said something to the moustache, and then the moustache said something to Daddy which made Daddy's face go very red, and then Daddy said something to Mummy, and Mummy – rather roughly – jerked Jeremy James's arm and led him away from the elephant house, leaving Daddy and the moustache talking together in loud voices.

'You must never,' said Mummy, 'never, never, never go through fences or try and touch the animals. You understand? They're very dangerous. You could have been killed!'

'Well I was only giving him a piece of bread he'd dropped,' said Jeremy James, 'and if he hadn't been such a stupid elephant, I wouldn't have had to get it for him.'

But there wasn't really much point in trying to explain it to Mummy, because she didn't have much clue about animals. Someone who prefers monkeys to elephants can't be expected to understand elephants – or little boys, if it comes to that.

CHAPTER SIX

Buried Treasure

At the bottom of the garden, right next to the fence that was so tall nobody could ever know what was on the other side, was a patch of land that belonged exclusively to Jeremy James. It wasn't a very big patch of land – because it wasn't a very big garden – but it was by far the most interesting place Jeremy James knew. And when the weather was fine he would often sit down on the ground and watch the ants collecting bits of insects, or the worms wriggling down into the earth, or the flies washing their hands, and he would wish that he was as tiny as they were so that he could recognize their faces and talk to them.

Mummy did give him some seeds once to plant, but nothing ever came of them, and the only thing that flourished on Jeremy James's land was what Daddy used to call flowers, and Mummy called weeds. Mummy said they should be torn up and thrown away, but Jeremy James thought they looked nice, and as it was *his* patch of land, he was allowed to keep them. Daddy thought he should keep them, too, because he said that Jeremy James didn't have to learn to weed at his age.

Now the night before the day we're talking about, Mummy had read Jeremy James a very exciting story about pirates, who used to rob people and then bury their treasure deep in the ground where nobody else could find it. (Daddy said they weren't called pirates any more, but tacksinspectus, or some funny name like that.) Jeremy James liked that story very much, and he reckoned that if there had been any pirates around where he lived, there was only one place they could possibly have chosen to bury their treasure and that was the most interesting place he knew. And so the next day – and next day is the day that we're talking about – he picked up his seaside spade and marched off to the bottom of the garden in search of fame and fortune.

The earth there wasn't quite as soft as the sand beside the sea, but pirates are clever people and don't bury their treasure where it's easy to find. Jeremy James knew that the harder it was, the more treasure there would be, and so he dug, and dug, and dug, and dug, until his arms and legs began to send complaints up to his head. Fouf, that's enough, they said, we arms and legs could do with a rest and a nice helping of strawberries and ice cream and fizzy lemonade and a bar of chocolate and a . . . but treasure-hunters' heads never take any notice of their arms and legs.

And just at the moment when the arms and legs were about to refuse to do any more digging for ever and ever, Jeremy James's seaside spade struck something very hard indeed.

'Gosh!' said Jeremy James, and brought his spade down on it again. It felt even harder the second time than the first. Jeremy James got down on his hands and knees, which had stopped sending complaints now, and scraped the earth off the treasure chest. It was certainly metal, and it was so hard the pirates must have put all their *best* jewels in it.

'Gosh!' said Jeremy James again, and started to dig all around the treasure chest, because he knew that even the biggest treasure in the world won't buy you many ice creams unless you can get it out of the ground. And so he dug, and then he pulled, and then he pushed, and he growled and he howled, and he hugged and he tugged, and he clasped and he gasped, and he sneezed and he wheezed . . . but the treasure

47

chest stayed exactly where it was, and never moved an inch.

Jeremy James sat down beside the treasure chest to have a good think. That was what Daddy always said – if you have a problem you should sit down and think about it. Mummy always said if you had a problem you should get up and do something about it, but Daddy said Mummy didn't understand these things, and so he carried on with his thinking and left Mummy to carry on with her doing. The funny thing was that by the time Daddy had finished his thinking, Mummy had usually finished her doing, and there wasn't much of a problem left for Daddy to deal with, but that never seemed to worry Daddy, because he said that only proved how much simpler life was if you sat down and had a good think while someone else was doing the doing.

Anyway, Jeremy James was a man like his Daddy, and so he sat next to his problem and thought about it. There was no way he could get that treasure chest out of the ground. So what could he do? He could, of course, tell Mummy and Daddy and ask them to help him, but this was *his* land and *his* treasure chest, and he wanted to show them, not them to show him. He didn't want to ask *anyone* for help. Treasure's treasure, and finding's keeping. But how do you get a treasure out of the ground if it refuses to come? Sometimes Jeremy James refused to come, and Mummy had ways of persuading him, but the treasure chest hadn't got ears to listen to a telling-off, and it hadn't got a bottom to feel a smack, so Mummy's methods certainly wouldn't work.

And then Jeremy James remembered something that had happened a long time ago. Picnic-time out in the green fields, with Daddy talking about the beauty of Nature and Mummy flapping a cloth at the flies and Jeremy James wishing they'd hurry up and bring out the ice cream. A tin of mandarin oranges, that's what Jeremy James was remembering now. A large tin for once, with a black label and a mouth-watering picture of mandarin oranges right in the middle. And Daddy saying, 'Just what I feel like – some nice juicy mandarin oranges – perfect end to a perfect meal. Eh, Jeremy James? How about some nice juicy mandarin oranges?' and Mummy saying, 'I forgot the tin-opener.' What happened then? Daddy said a few words, and Mummy said she was sorry, and then Daddy sat down to think, and what did Mummy do? She got a knife out of the bag, held the tin very firmly on the ground, and pushed the point of the knife right through the top of the tin. Then she waggled it around until there was a hole big enough for all that sweet, cool, juicy treasure to come pouring out. That was the way to do it. Get something with a sharp point, waggle it around, and out would come all the sparkling gold and silver.

Jeremy James looked down the garden towards the living-room window, the kitchen window, the bedroom window, the bathroom window. Not a Mummy or a Daddy in sight. A quick dash across the lawn, and he was safe inside Daddy's tool shed.

And inside Daddy's tool shed he soon found just what he was looking for. It was a lot bigger than a knife, and it had a great big handle and a big round pointed head, and Jeremy James could hardly lift it, it was so heavy. But one thump with that, and the treasure would be his for sure. Another quick look down the garden, and then Jeremy James wrestled the pickaxe back across the lawn to the earthy cradle of his golden future.

The pickaxe really was very heavy, but Jeremy James was very determined, and a determined boy and a heavy pickaxe can do quite a lot of damage to a stubborn stick-in-the-mud treasure chest. There was a loud clang as pickaxe and treasure chest were introduced to each other, and Jeremy James bent down to have a look. He hadn't managed to break through yet, but there was a nice deep dent in the metal – and after all, pirates don't bury their gold and silver in mandarin orange tins. One more thump on the same place should do it. The pickaxe wobbled up into the air again, and crashed down into the earth beside the treasure chest, giving one wriggling pink worm a terrible shock that sent it squirming in all directions at once. 'Missed!' said Jeremy James, and gathered strength for another attack. Three times the pickaxe rose and fell, and by the third stroke there wasn't a worm in sight, but Jeremy James was not to be put off. He took very very careful aim, drew in enough air to float half a dozen Christmas balloons, and heaved the pickaxe up to the sky once more. When it came down, there was a glorious crunch as the point pierced the metal, and then a very strange thing happened. There was a great whoosh, and something shot high into the air, and when it came down again it was very wet, and Jeremy James found himself being drenched with the coldest, heaviest shower he'd ever been showered with.

'Mummy!' he shouted, and dripped hastily across the lawn to the French doors, which opened even before he could shout 'Mummy!' again.

Ever such a lot of things happened during the next hour or so. There were phone calls and running backwards and forwards, and The Men came, and Jeremy James was sent to his room, and Daddy had a talk with a big man who had a red face and a bristly moustache, and some of the neighbours knocked on the front door, and The Men kept tramping in and out, and when Jeremy James went to the lavatory it wouldn't flush, and when he told Mummy the lavatory wouldn't flush she smacked his bottom and told him to go back to his room, and in the end, when everyone had gone, the garden looked like a paddling pool and the house was full of muddy boot-marks which Mummy said were Jeremy James's fault, though the feet were obviously a hundred times bigger than his. And Daddy came upstairs, and sat with Jeremy James on the bed, and put on a very serious, very Daddy-like voice, and told him that he must never, never take the pickaxe again, or go digging again, or go 'messing up the whole caboodle again' – which was very unfair since Jeremy James didn't even know what a caboodle was. And Mummy said

51

he should go to bed without any supper, but Daddy brought him a sandwich and said he'd jolly well better not make any crumbs. And goodnight and God bless.

Jeremy James sat up in bed and munched his sandwich (which was strawberry jam – his favourite) and reflected on the injustices of the world he lived in. Of course, all that water must have caused a lot of trouble, but he'd got as wet as anybody, and it shouldn't have needed much common sense for them to realize that it wasn't his fault. After all, they'd have been pleased enough if he'd come in with his pockets full of gold and silver. Why on earth should they blame him if those stupid pirates had gone and buried a box of water instead?

CHAPTER SEVEN

The Doctor

Jeremy James wasn't very well. In the night he'd had to call for Mummy, and he'd been very sick – horribly smelly sick, all over the bedclothes. And Mummy had had to stroke his hair, and sit by him for a while, which was rather nice. And the crispy clean sheets were rather nice, too. But being ill wasn't so nice, especially the being sick part, which was very un-nice. Even Daddy had come in for a few minutes while Jeremy James was being sick – and it took a lot to get Daddy out of bed for *anything* – but Mummy said he looked even worse than Jeremy James felt, so he should go back to bed. And Daddy said something like, 'Worple doctor semantics', and Mummy said, 'In the morning', and Daddy said, 'Semantics doctor worple', and Jeremy James said, 'Gloop!' and Daddy went away very quickly and Mummy stayed with Jeremy James.

Now that it was morning, Jeremy James felt a bit better. He didn't feel all better, but just sort of better better. He felt better enough to get up and play, but not better enough to eat his cornflakes and drink his milk. Anyway, Mummy said he wasn't better

enough to get up and play either, so he stayed in bed and Mummy phoned for the doctor. When Mummy came back from phoning, she was holding a little packet in her hand. It was a cardboard packet, with lots of bright colours on it, and Jeremy James knew even before Mummy said anything just which packet it was and where Mummy had found it.

'Now then,' said Mummy ... and this wasn't Mummy's are-you-feeling-better-darling voice at all ... 'last night, Jeremy James, when I changed your pillow, I found this. And it's empty.'

'Yes,' said Jeremy James.

'A big box of liquorice allsorts,' said Mummy.

'Er ... hmmph!' said Jeremy James.

'I suppose you ate them all,' said Mummy.

'Oh yes,' said Jeremy James. 'Nobody helped me.'

'After you'd cleaned your teeth,' said Mummy.

'Hmmph,' said Jeremy James.

'And then,' said Mummy, 'you were sick.'

'Well no,' said Jeremy James, 'I wasn't sick *then*. I wasn't, Mummy, not *then*.'

'Oh?' said Mummy.

'I didn't feel at all sick *then*. I went to sleep, that's what I did *then*.'

'Jeremy James,' said Mummy, 'you must never, never eat sweets before you go to sleep. You must never eat anything after you've cleaned your teeth. And you must never, never, never eat a whole box of liquorice allsorts at one go. Do you hear?'

'Yes, Mummy,' said Jeremy James.

'One liquorice allsort, or maybe two,' said Mummy, 'and that's enough.'

'Yes, Mummy,' said Jeremy James, though inside he said to himself that one liquorice allsort, or maybe two, wasn't enough and never could be enough, and only a grown-up would ever imagine that it *was* enough, because only grown-ups liked little helpings of nice things and big helpings of nasty things. Mummy would never say for instance, 'One potato, or maybe two, and that's enough', or one cornflake, or one carrot, or one cabbage leaf. Oh no, you could have as many of those things as you liked (or didn't like). But ask for more mandarin oranges, more chocolate, more liquorice allsorts, and all you'd get was the no-more-they're-not-good-for-you speech.

Dr Bassett was the tallest man in the world. He

was taller than the house, because when he came into Jeremy James's room, he had to bend down so that his head wouldn't go through the roof. He was taller than the apple tree, because the apple tree wasn't as tall as the house, and so he must have been taller than Daddy, because Daddy couldn't reach the top of the apple tree, except when he borrowed Mr Robertson's ladder, and even then he usually couldn't get to the top of the apple tree because either he or the ladder kept falling down. Dr Bassett was a very tall man.

'Well now, old chap,' said Dr Bassett, 'how are we feeling?'

'Who?' asked Jeremy James.

'You,' said Dr Bassett.

'Oh,' said Jeremy James. 'I'm very well, thank you, and I've been sick.'

'Ah,' said Dr Bassett.

'He ate a whole box of liquorice allsorts before he went to bed,' said Mummy.

'It wasn't before I went to bed,' said Jeremy James, 'it was after I went to bed.'

'Ah,' said Dr Bassett, 'that does make a difference.'

Dr Bassett had a very interesting-looking black bag, which was full of chocolate, tins of fruit, toy soldiers, toy guns and railway engines, until he opened it, and then it was full of very boring things like youknowwhats and whatdoyoucallits. Jeremy James was poked with a youknowwhat, and pulled a face, then he was tickled with a whatdoyoucallit, and giggled. Then Dr Bassett looked into his mouth, felt his head, tapped his chest and ruffled his hair.

'He'll be all right,' said Dr Bassett.

'No I won't,' said Jeremy James. 'Because I'm not ill where you were looking and you were looking in the wrong place.'

'Ah,' said Dr Bassett.

'Jeremy James!' said Mummy.

'And where should I have looked?' asked Dr Bassett.

'In my tummy,' said Jeremy James. 'That's where I'm ill, 'cos that's where the pain was.'

'Of course,' said Dr Bassett. 'Aren't I a silly old doctor, not looking in your tummy? Let's have a look at it then.'

And Dr Bassett had a very close look at Jeremy James's tummy. He bent right over like the beanstalk must have done when Jack chopped it, and Jeremy James could see through his grey hair and on to his shiny head, and Dr Bassett pointed his little torch on to Jeremy James's tummy, and studied the tummy for a very long time.

'Well,' said Dr Bassett, 'you were quite right, Jeremy James. There's a pink liquorice allsort in there, and it's been having a fight with a blue liquorice allsort, and that's what all the trouble was about. If you'd just eaten a blue liquorice allsort, or you'd just eaten a pink one, they couldn't have had a fight, and you wouldn't have been ill. It's a good thing you told me to look, isn't it?'

'Yes,' said Jeremy James.

'Anyway,' said Dr Bassett, turning to Mummy, 'he's got a little bit of a temperature. It's probably a touch of flu, as a matter of fact. I should keep him in bed for a day or two, and just give him plenty of liquids. He'll soon let you know himself when he's better. I'll write you out a prescription . . .'

Now this was all very strange. Because Dr Bassett had been to the house before. And the last time Dr Bassett had come to the house, it hadn't been to see Jeremy James, but to see Daddy because Daddy had been dying, and dying very loudly, with a lot of 'foofs' and 'phaws' and 'hmmphs' and 'aaahs'. And Dr Bassett had Jack-in-the-beanstalked over Daddy, too, and poked him and tickled him, and Daddy had said something about it being the end, and Dr Bassett had said it wasn't quite the end, but it was . . . it definitely was . . . it most certainly was . . . a touch of flu. And if Daddy had a touch of flu then, and Jeremy James had a touch of flu now . . . It was all very complicated, but Jeremy James managed to work it out just before Dr Bassett folded himself in two to get through the door.

'Excuse me,' said Jeremy James, because that was what you always said to grown-ups when you wanted them to turn and look at you.

'Yes, old chap?' asked Dr Bassett, turning to look at Jeremy James.

'Can you,' asked Jeremy James, 'get a touch of flu through eating too many liquorice allsorts?'

'Ah,' said Dr Bassett. 'I'll have to ask the Royal

Society to look into that one. But as far as I know, most people find a different way of getting it.'

'Well, did my Daddy get it through eating too many liquorice allsorts?' asked Jeremy James.

Dr Bassett seven-league-booted back to the bed, and whispered very, very secretly: 'That's highly problematical. You see, it's only very clever people that get a touch of flu through eating too many liquorice allsorts. Now, do you think that's how you got yours?'

Jeremy James had a quick think, because you have to have a quick think before you answer a question like that.

'Well,' said Jeremy James, 'I think that maybe I possibly might have done.'

'I think you possibly might have done as well,' said Dr Bassett.

And Jeremy James sat back in his bed and tried to work out whether it was better to be clever and eat liquorice allsorts and get a touch of flu, or not to be clever and not to eat liquorice allsorts and not to get a touch of flu. The best thing might be to be clever and to eat liquorice allsorts and not to get a touch of flu, but Dr Bassett had already gone, and it was too late to ask him whether anyone possibly might have been clever enough to do that.

CHAPTER EIGHT

Timothy

Timothy lived next door, and he was Jeremy James's best friend, and Jeremy James didn't like him very much. The trouble with Timothy was that he was spoilt, and anything Jeremy James had, Timothy had too but even more so. If Jeremy James had a train set to go round the living room, Timothy had a train set to go round the living room *and* the dining room *and* the hall. If Jeremy James had a tricycle with a bell, Timothy had a tricycle with a bell *and* a hooter *and* a saddlebag. And if Jeremy James went to the zoo on a Saturday, Timothy had already been there on Friday, which was the only day when the elephants were allowed to escape and little boys were allowed to ride on them.

Timothy was one year older than Jeremy James, and he was taller, fatter, stronger, richer. Timothy had red hair, and told Jeremy James over and over again that red hair was the best thing anyone could have on top of his head. Timothy had freckles on his face, and as everyone knows, a face without freckles can hardly be called a face. But worst of all, Timothy went to school, and anyone who hasn't been to school simply doesn't know what life is all about. Timothy did all kinds of marvellous things at school, like eating all day long, teaching the teachers how to do reading and writing, making pictures which were the best pictures anyone had ever made because his Daddy said so, and fighting ten boys at a time and knocking them all out with a single punch. Timothy knew everything, could do everything, had done everything.

Timothy had a great big tent in which he and Jeremy James could play Indians. Jeremy James had a tent, too, but there was only room for one Indian in his tent. Timothy's tent could hold a tribe. And so they always played Indians in Timothy's tent in Timothy's garden, which was bigger than Jeremy James's garden. Timothy was always the chief – after all, it was *his* tent and *his* garden – and Jeremy James was either a miserable Indian tied to a stake ready for painful torture and eventual head-cutting-off, or he was a miserable cowboy awaiting the same fate. The only time Jeremy James was allowed to torture and cut off heads was if little Billy from over the road came and played with them, or his baby sister Gillian, but they were so small that you couldn't really enjoy cutting their heads off because it was too easy. Anyway they didn't know you were doing it, and as they didn't know, they didn't scream, and cutting heads off without the scream is like eating strawberries without the cream.

Now the first Sunday after Jeremy James had been in bed with liquorice allsort flu, he and Timothy were out in Timothy's tent, and Jeremy James had just had his head cut off for the twentieth time.

'Can I cut your head off now?' asked Jeremy James.

'No,' said Timothy. 'It's my tent.'

'It's not fair,' said Jeremy James for the twenty-first time.

'And it's my garden, too,' said Timothy.

'Well let's go and play in my tent in my garden,' said Jeremy James.

'Your tent's too small,' said Timothy, 'and if we don't play here then I'm not playing at all. And I'm older than you and I'm bigger than you.'

All of which was very true.

'Well, I've had flu,' said Jeremy James, which was also true but didn't really have a great deal to do with the question under discussion.

'I know,' said Timothy. 'I had flu when I was your age but I've grown out of it now.'

'You can't grow out of flu,' said Jeremy James, ''cos my Daddy's had it – the doctor said.'

'I know,' said Timothy, 'but that's different – the flu that grown-ups get can't be grown out of. I learnt all about it at school. There's grown-up flu, and other flu.'

'Well I had the same as Daddy,' said Jeremy James.

'You didn't,' said Timothy.

'I did,' said Jeremy James.

And after five minutes of I-did-you-didn'ting, Timothy jumped on Jeremy James and cut off his head for the twenty-first time and as far as he was concerned, that proved that Jeremy James didn't have grown-up flu.

Now Jeremy James was certainly smaller than Timothy, and younger, and not so richly endowed with experience of the great big world outside, but Jeremy James was also very determined. And what was even more important – he was right, and Timothy was wrong. So when the Great Apache Chief had got off his victim and lowered his bloodstained tomahawk, Jeremy James scrambled to his feet and informed his tormentor that not only was he, Jeremy James, right, but also he, Timothy, was wrong, and he, Jeremy James' could prove that he, Timothy, had not grown out of flu at all but could be given the *same* flu as he, Jeremy James, had so recently fought and conquered. The *same*. And he, Jeremy James, could prove it.

'You can't,' said Timothy.

'I can,' said Jeremy James. ' 'Cos I know what I got it from – I got it from a special medicine, and you'll get the same flu if you take the medicine, so there.'

'I won't,' said Timothy.

'You will,' said Jeremy James.

'Prove it,' said Timothy.

At this moment, Jeremy James had a vague feeling that he should have reached for his six-shooter and shot Timothy through the chest, but he hadn't got his six-shooter with him.

'Wait here,' he said, leapt on his horse, and galloped at breakneck speed through the gap in the fence, across the lawn, through the back door, through the living room, up the stairs, and into his own bedroom. And there, in a very very secret place which no one must ever mention on pain of having his head cut off, Jeremy James uncovered his treasure chest and, from the pile of biscuits, cakes, sweets and chocolate which no one must ever mention on pain of being tied to a stake and tortured to death, he extracted a large brightly coloured box. Then he put his treasure chest back in the very very secret place, leapt on to his horse, and galloped at breakneck speed out of his bedroom, down the stairs, through the living room, through the back door, across the lawn, through the gap in the fence, and into Timothy's tent.

'Here,' said Jeremy James. 'Flu medicine.'

'I know what those are,' said Timothy. 'They're liquorice allsorts.'

'They may look like liquorice allsorts,' said Jeremy James, 'but they're really flu medicine, and you've got to eat them all, and you'll get flu just like the flu I had and Daddy had and it's the *same* flu.'

'You can't get flu from liquorice allsorts,' said Timothy.

'Oh yes you can,' said Jeremy James, ' 'cos the doctor said so, but you just have to be clever to get it, that's all, and maybe you're not clever enough.'

Now Timothy knew you couldn't get flu from eating liquorice allsorts, because that was just the sort of thing he'd learned at school. But Timothy rather liked liquorice allsorts, and it wasn't every day of the week that somebody put a whole box of liquorice allsorts in your hand and actually *told* you to eat them, and even though he was a very great Indian chief, and Jeremy James was only a miserable Indian or a miserable cowboy, a box of liquorice allsorts was a box of liquorice allsorts, and this was a very big box of liquorice allsorts, and ... well ...

'All right,' said Timothy, 'I'll show you.'

And he showed Jeremy James. One after another he gobbled up the flu medicine allsorts – pink ones, black ones, blue ones, stripy ones, square ones ...

'Maybe I should just have one ...' said Jeremy James.

'No,' said Timothy, 'you gave them to me so they're mine, and anyway it's my tent and my garden.'

Which was true.

And down went the liquorice allsorts, and the packet got emptier and emptier, and Timothy's mouth got blacker and blacker, and Jeremy James got hungrier and hungrier.

'There you are,' said Timothy, 'all gone. And I haven't got flu, you see. I told you I wouldn't.'

'Hmmph,' said Jeremy James.

Then they buried the packet as if it was a bone, and hurried off obediently in answer to a double Mummy call of 'Tea-time!' Jeremy James hurried considerably more hurriedly than Timothy. In fact Timothy couldn't really be said to have hurried at all – he sort of unhurried to the house, as if he had something very heavy inside which had slipped down to his feet and made them difficult to lift.

That evening Mummy spotted Dr Bassett's car from the window.

'That's funny,' said Mummy. 'Someone must be ill next door – I've just seen the doctor go in.'

'I know,' said Jeremy James. 'It's Timothy. He's got flu.'

'How do you know that, dear?' said Mummy.

'Hmmph,' said Jeremy James, and gave a little smile as he beheaded a toy solder.

CHAPTER NINE

The Bathroom Lock

Daddy had been going to mend the bathroom lock straightaway for about two weeks now. Practically every day Mummy had said to him, 'I do wish you'd get that bathroom lock fixed, dear,' and Daddy had said, 'I'll do it straightaway – as soon as I've finished this.' And this, which had also been that, those and the others, always kept Daddy fully occupied until lunch, tea, supper or bedtime. Thus the bathroom lock remained well and truly unmended, and every morning, when Jeremy James went to do his Number Two, Mummy had to say to him, 'Don't lock the bathroom door, Jeremy James,' and Jeremy James would say, 'Why not?' and Mummy would say, 'Because it hasn't been mended yet,' and Daddy would say, 'I'll get that seen to straightaway – as soon as I've finished this.'

But one morning, Mummy forgot to say to Jeremy James, 'Don't lock the bathroom door, Jeremy James,' and Jeremy James locked it. As soon as he'd locked it, he remembered that he shouldn't have locked it, and he waited for the house to fall down, but it didn't, and so he sat down to do his Number Two, and wondered what all the fuss had been about.

'Hurry up in there,' said Mummy, when Jeremy James had only been sitting there for a quarter of a minute.

'I'm doing my Number Two!' said Jeremy James. These things can't always be hurried.

However, this morning was a nice sunny morning, which should be good for climbing and tricycling and – with a bit of luck – strawberry and creaming, so Jeremy James quickly broke the world record for sheets of toilet paper, washed his hands with the nice-smelling soap that nobody but Mummy was allowed to use, and pulled open the bathroom door. That is to say, he pulled the bathroom door to what should have been open, but the bathroom door had other ideas and stayed shut. 'Ah,' said Jeremy James, 'it's locked, that's why,' and so he turned the key. That is to say, he pulled the key to what should have been a turn, but the key only went halfway round and then refused to move another inch. 'Come on, key,' said Jeremy James, but the key wouldn't come on, round, or out. It simply stayed where it was – like the Grand Old Duke of York's Men, neither up nor down.

'Mummy,' said Jeremy James. 'Mummy! Mummy!'

'Did you call, Jeremy James?'

'I'm stuck in the bathroom!'

Silence. Thump, thump, up the stairs. Creak, creak, as Mummy pushed the bathroom door, and the bathroom door pushed back.

'You locked it, did you?' said Mummy through the locked door.

'I forgot,' said Jeremy James.

'John!' shouted Mummy. 'John! John!'

'Did you call, dear?'

'Jeremy James is stuck in the bathroom!'

Silence. Thump, thump, up the stairs. Creak, creak, as Daddy pushed the bathroom door, and the bathroom door pushed back.

'You locked it, did you?' said Daddy through the locked door.

'Of course he locked it,' said Mummy. 'Otherwise he wouldn't be stuck, would he?'

There was a long silence outside the bathroom door. Daddy must have been thinking.

'Is anybody there?' asked Jeremy James.

'It's all right,' said Daddy. 'I'm thinking. Now don't worry, we'll soon get you out of there. Don't worry, son. Just keep calm.'

'I was only wondering if anybody was there,' said Jeremy James.

'Now listen,' said Daddy. 'I'm going to pull the door. And when I tell you, I want you to try and turn the key. Do you understand?'

'Yes,' said Jeremy James.

The door creaked.

'Now!' said Daddy. And Jeremy James's hand turned, but the key stayed where it was.

'It's not moving,' said Jeremy James.

'All right,' said Daddy. 'Now don't worry, I'll soon get you out.'

'You'll have to get a ladder,' said Mummy.

'Wait a moment,' said Daddy. 'Jeremy James, can you get the key out of the lock?'

'No,' said Jeremy James.

'Well try,' said Daddy.

Jeremy James tried.

'No,' said Jeremy James.

'You'll have to get a ladder,' said Mummy.

'Now look,' said Daddy. 'I'll pull the door again, and when I tell you, try turning the key *the other way*. You understand? Try and turn it the other way – the way you weren't turning it before.'

'All right,' said Jeremy James.

'Now,' said Daddy.

And Jeremy James's hand turned the other way, but the key stayed where it was.

'It's not moving,' said Jeremy James.

'You'll have to get a ladder,' said Mummy.

'Now don't worry, son,' said Daddy. 'We'll soon get you out. Maybe I'd better go and get a ladder.'

'Mrs Robertson opposite has got a big ladder. She's usually in at this time.'

'You stay here, then,' said Daddy. 'Keep talking to him – you know, calm him down. Child must be scared stiff. Which are the Robertsons?'

'Number 14, over the road.'

'Is their name Robertson? I thought they were the Wilkinsons.'

'The Wilkinsons are Number 16. Do go and get the ladder, dear.'

'All right, Jeremy James,' said Daddy. 'I'm just going to get a ladder from the Wilkinsons.'

'The Robertsons.'

'. . . the Robertsons, and I'll be back in half a minute. You keep calm, son, we'll soon have you out of there. You're all right, aren't you?'

'Yes, thank you, Daddy.'

'Nothing to worry about.'

And there was a thump thump clatter crash, as Daddy raced down the first dozen stairs and fell down the rest.

'Jeremy James,' said Mummy, 'is the bathroom window open?'

'No,' said Jeremy James, 'it's shut.'

'Do you think you can open it?'

'Yes, I think so,' said Jeremy James. 'I can climb on the bath.'

'Then open it, only be very careful,' said Mummy. 'Mind you don't fall.'

Jeremy James climbed up on the edge of the bath, and then stepped very carefully across to the other side. He was being very brave. After all, it's not every day you have to step across a cliff that's a thousand foot high with hundreds of crocodiles waiting down below with great big open jaws and rumbling tummies. Jeremy James balanced on the edge of the bath, and held on to the towel rail to make sure he didn't turn into crocodile breakfast. Then he reached up, and with a flick of his hero's hand, turned the catch that would save the world.

Through the open window he could peep down into the garden below. It was quite a long way down, and if you fell from there you'd certainly be killed.

'Have you got it open?' asked Mummy.

'Yes,' said Jeremy James, 'and it's ever such a long way down to the garden, and if I fell from here I'd be killed.'

'Now you be careful!' said Mummy. 'Keep right away from the window!'

'You keep calm!' said Jeremy James. 'Don't worry, I'll be all right.'

And just then there was a scratchy scrapy sound against the wall as Daddy persuaded the ladder to stand up against it. Then there was a bumpy bouncy sound as the top part of the ladder decided it would rather be with the bottom part of the ladder, and went racing down the wall, just missing Daddy, who had managed to jump aside at the last moment. Daddy then let out one or two of the words Jeremy James must *never never* use, and there was a long silence.

Jeremy James peeped out of the window.

'Daddy's hurt himself,' said Jeremy James.

Mummy thump-thumped down the stairs and out into the garden, and Jeremy James leaned out of the window to look at Mummy looking at Daddy.

'I'll just get you a plaster,' Mummy was saying, and Daddy was saying, 'Blooming ladder . . . death trap . . . worple worple semantics,' and things like that.

'Are you all right?' said Jeremy James.

'You get back in, and keep away from the window!' said Daddy. 'It's all your fault in the first place!'

'If you'd mended the lock when . . .' Jeremy James missed the rest of what Mummy was saying, because he'd stepped back from the window, forgotten where he was, and gone tumbling a thousand foot down into the watery jaws of the bathtub. By the time he'd killed twenty crocodiles – which took him at least twenty seconds – the ladder was up the wall and Daddy was up the ladder, his white face peering through the open window.

'Jeremy James, Jeremy James, are you all right?'

Jeremy James finished off the twenty-first crocodile, and scrambled victoriously to his feet. 'Hello, Daddy.'

'Are you all right, son?'

'Yes, thank you.'

With a heave and a grunt and a fouf and a few of those words, Daddy squeezed himself across the window-ledge and down head first into the bath, followed by a shower of bottles, toothpaste, sponges and motor boats. Fortunately the crocodiles were all dead by now, or Daddy really would have been in trouble.

'Are you all right, Daddy?' asked Jeremy James.

Daddy got his head up where his feet had been, and put his feet down where his head had been, and then gave Jeremy James a funny look. 'Yes,' he said. 'Apart from a broken arm, a broken leg and a broken neck. And how are you?'

'Not too bad, thank you,' said Jeremy James. 'But the crocodiles *nearly* got me.'

'Crocodiles in the bath, eh?' said Daddy.

'But I killed them all in the end.'

'Good,' said Daddy. 'I'm in no condition to fight crocodiles.'

Then Daddy got the bathroom door unlocked, and Mummy gave Jeremy James a big hug and a big kiss and promised him ice cream for dinner because he'd been so brave, and Jeremy James said it was nothing, and he wouldn't mind being locked in the bathroom every day, and Daddy took the ladder back to the Robertsons, and Mummy gave Jeremy James a sweet, and Daddy came back from the Robertsons, and Mummy said to Daddy, 'Hadn't you better go and mend that lock now?' and Daddy said, 'I'll just get some plaster on this hand,' and Mummy said,

'Hmmph.' But Daddy really did mend the lock as soon as he'd put the plaster on his hand. And when he'd finished mending the lock, he had to put some plaster on the other hand as well. Daddy always used a lot of plaster when he was mending things.

CHAPTER TEN

The Babysitter

Mummy and Daddy were going out. They were going to what Mummy called a 'do' and Daddy called a 'worple worple nuisance', and it meant that they had to put on very smart clothes, and Daddy would be ready very early and Mummy would be ready very late. So Jeremy James and the babysitter sat in the living room, and Daddy kept walking up and down, looking at his watch, and shouting, 'Come on, dear, we'll be late!' and Mummy kept calling out, 'Just coming!' and didn't come. And then she did come, and Daddy said, 'Don't you look lovely!' and 'That was certainly worth waiting for!' and kissed her. Then he said, 'We'll be late,' and Mummy said, 'The place won't run away,' and she gave Jeremy James a nice kiss and she smelt just like a queen. When Mummy and Daddy went out, they seemed quite different somehow.

While Daddy stood outside the front door, Mummy told the babysitter when Jeremy James was to go to bed, what she was to do if he said he wouldn't go to bed, where to find the tea, the biscuits and the cake, how the television worked, what number to phone if the house caught fire, where she had bought that lovely green tablecloth, what time they would be back ... 'Come on, dear!' said Daddy, from miles away. 'Coming!' said Mummy – and ten minutes later, they were gone.

The babysitter was rather old – she must have been at least seventeen – and she had black hair and glasses and a soft voice. Jeremy James liked her soft voice, because he couldn't imagine a soft voice like that ever saying, 'Jeremy James, do as you're told!' or 'Jeremy James, put those sweets away this minute!' or 'Jeremy James, you must go to bed immediately!' A soft voice like that would certainly say, 'Um ... would you mind ...' and would keep quiet if you said you *would* mind. Jeremy James liked babysitters with soft voices.

'Are you sleepy yet?' asked the soft voice.

'No,' said Jeremy James, 'but I'm hungry.'

The babysitter went into the kitchen and came back with a plate of cakes and biscuits which were cakier and biskier than any of the old cakes and biscuits Jeremy James was given for tea.

'Would you like one of these?' asked the babysitter, and Jeremy James proceeded to like rather more than one of these, and the babysitter never said a word.

'Now what would you like to do?' asked the babysitter, when Jeremy James had finished the cakes and biscuits.

Nobody had ever before asked Jeremy James what he would *like* to do. He'd been told what he ought to like to do, and he'd been told what he had to do, and he'd been told what he shouldn't have done – but what he would *like* to do, that was something quite new. It needed to be thought about very carefully, and so he sat in his chair, licking the chocolate ring round his mouth, and thought about it very carefully. What would he *really* like to do? With the whole world suddenly open to him, with everything allowed, with a choice that was his and his alone . . . what *would* he like to do?

'I'd like to play hide-and-seek,' said Jeremy James, and the pearly gates of paradise opened before him. 'Hide-and-seek,' he said, *'that's* what I'd like to do.'

'All right,' said the babysitter, 'who's going to hide, you or me?'

'I'll hide,' said Jeremy James, 'and you must close your eyes and count up to a hundred. And you mustn't open your eyes, because that's called cheating.'

And so the babysitter closed her eyes, and Jeremy James tiptoed upstairs and crept into Mummy and Daddy's room and dived into Mummy and Daddy's bed, which he wasn't ever supposed to dive into, but which it was all right to dive into now, because he was playing hide-and-seek with the babysitter, and that was official. And it was lovely and soft and warm in Mummy and Daddy's bed, even though Mummy and Daddy weren't in it, and Jeremy James curled up and listened for the footsteps of the babysitter. Thump, thump she came up the stairs, and Jeremy James giggled because she'd never think of looking

in Mummy and Daddy's bedroom, and thump thump came the steps, straight into Mummy and Daddy's bedroom, on went the light, and 'Caught you!' said the babysitter, and 'That's not fair!' said Jeremy James. 'You cheated! You opened your eyes!' 'I heard you laughing!' said the babysitter. 'Well it's not fair,' said Jeremy James. 'You weren't supposed to listen.'

But the babysitter *had* listened, and the babysitter had caught him, and now, she insisted, it was her turn to hide and Jeremy James would have to look for her, and he must close his eyes and count up to a hundred.

'Well I can't,' said Jeremy James, 'I can only count up to twenty-ten, so there!'

But Jeremy James did close his eyes. Then the babysitter left the room, and Jeremy James opened his eyes again, because after all if it was fair for her to listen then it was fair for him to look. So he tiptoed to the door, peeped out, and saw the babysitter disappearing into the bathroom.

'Nineteen, twenty, twenty-ten, a hundred,' said Jeremy James, 'and here I come.' And he went straight to the bathroom, opened the door, said, 'Caught you!' and then looked for the babysitter. But there was no babysitter to be seen. 'Oh!' said Jeremy James, and went out of the bathroom. 'That's funny,' said Jeremy James. Then he looked in the bathroom again, but there was still no babysitter.

'Where are you?' said Jeremy James.

He had a good look in the bath, but she was definitely not in it, and he had a look in the bathroom stool, but she wasn't in that either. And she wasn't in the airing cupboard and she wasn't down the lavatory.

'I know where you are,' said Jeremy James, but that didn't make the babysitter appear either. 'I don't know where you are,' said Jeremy James. 'Where are you?' said Jeremy James. And then he went out on to the landing, into Mummy and Daddy's room, into his own room, into the guest room, and he opened all the cupboards and all the drawers, and he looked in all the beds, and he looked under all the beds, and he looked behind all the beds . . . but there was still no babysitter. And he decided that hide-and-seek really wasn't so much fun after all, and it would be better to play something else, and the babysitter was cheating and it only went to prove that you couldn't play proper games with girls, even if they were official girls like the babysitter.

'Where are you?' he said. 'Come out, I don't want to play any more, I give up, it's a silly game . . .' etc. etc. and at last the babysitter came into view as she stepped out from behind the bathroom door.

'Caught you!' said Jeremy James, but he wasn't really convinced of that himself. 'Anyway, that was a silly place to hide . . . it's not fair to hide there . . . it's my turn . . . you must close your eyes . . .'

'I thought you didn't want to play hide-and-seek any more,' said the babysitter.

'Well, just once more,' said Jeremy James. 'I'll hide and you count up to a hundred. And you mustn't open your eyes.'

So the babysitter went back into the bathroom and closed her eyes, and Jeremy James padded downstairs, thinking very very hard. This time he'd find a really *good* place to hide, somewhere she'd never *think* of looking, the best hiding place anyone had ever found in the whole world. But where?

Jeremy James crept into the kitchen. Where?

Jeremy James looked at the kitchen windows. Jeremy James looked at the kitchen door. Jeremy James opened the kitchen door, giggled, stepped out into the twilit garden, and softly closed the kitchen door behind him. Then ever so quietly he tiptoed across the lawn, opened the door to Daddy's tool shed, squeezed in, and closed the door again. She'd never find him here, and that was a fact. Jeremy James giggled. She could open her eyes now, *and* she

could listen if she wanted to – but she wouldn't find him.

Jeremy James curled up in a deckchair, and pulled an old rug over himself. It wasn't as soft or as warm as Mummy and Daddy's bed, but it was *quite* soft and it was *quite* warm, and it was rather cosy in the tool shed, and she'd certainly never find him there, and hide-and-seek was a nice game after all, and she wasn't bad company for a girl, and she was a lot better than some of the babysitters that had looked after him, and she had a quiet voice, and . . . and . . . and . . . Jeremy James fell fast asleep.

A lot of things happened that night. First of all, Mummy and Daddy came home from the 'do' much earlier than expected. They came home because they'd had a phone call from the babysitter, who'd sounded very upset and rather frightened. Then there were some policemen who came in a big blue car, and *they* came because *they'd* had a phone call from Daddy, who'd sounded very upset and rather frightened. And some of the neighbours came to the house, because Mummy had knocked on their doors, and Mummy had sounded very upset and rather frightened. But Jeremy James didn't know about all this, because he was fast asleep, minding his own business in Daddy's tool shed. It wasn't until he was carried into the house in the arms of a great big policeman with a red face and a bristling moustache that Jeremy James began to take notice of all the activity around him, but even then he was very sleepy and couldn't quite make up his mind whether the policeman was real or just part of a funny dream. Then he was passed across to Daddy's arms and he heard Mummy's voice, and he opened his eyes wide because it sounded as if Mummy was crying. And it really was Mummy and she really was crying, and he really was in Daddy's arms, and there really was a great big policeman there, and lots of other people were there, too, and over in a corner was the babysitter, and she looked as if she was crying as well.

'Oh, hello,' said Jeremy James. 'You didn't find me, did you?'

Then the policeman with the red face and bristling moustache said he'd like a word with Daddy, and Daddy said maybe Jeremy James had better go to bed, and so Jeremy James was passed to Mummy, and Mummy carried him up the stairs to his bed, tucked him in, looked at him for a very long time, and then kissed him goodnight.

'Mummy,' said Jeremy James, 'I had ever such a nice time with the babysitter. Can she come here again to look after me?'

'Hmmph,' said Mummy. 'Well as a matter of fact, I don't think she *will* be coming again, Jeremy James.'

'Oh Mummy, why not?' said Jeremy James.

'Because . . .' said Mummy, '. . . because she's not very good at hide-and-seek, that's why.'

And Mummy was right because the babysitter didn't come again. And Daddy put a lock on the tool shed, which was something he'd been meaning to do for ages.

CHAPTER ELEVEN

A Death in the Family

Great-Aunt Maud was dead. She was Mummy's Great-Aunt Maud, which made her Jeremy James's Great-Great-Aunt Maud, but Jeremy James didn't know her anyway, so as far as he was concerned, it didn't matter whether she was Great, Great-Great, or Not-So-Great. What was much more impressive was the fact that she was ninety-two when she died.

'Ninety-two!' said Jeremy James, when he heard the news. 'But that's enormously old! That's hundreds of years old! That's even older than Daddy!'

Mummy held the letter in her hand, and shed a few tears.

'I don't know what you're crying about,' said Daddy. 'We never could stand her. She was a silly old woman.'

'But she's dead,' said Mummy.

'Well then, she's a dead silly old woman,' said Daddy. 'Look at all the trouble she caused before we got married.'

'That's all in the past,' said Mummy. 'And you shouldn't speak ill of the dead.'

'It doesn't hurt the dead as much as it hurts the living,' said Daddy, 'and that's a fact.'

The funeral was on Saturday. Daddy said he would stay at home and look after Jeremy James, but Mummy said he wouldn't and Jeremy James would have to go as well. Then Daddy said he wouldn't go whatever happened, and Mummy said he was being childish, and Daddy said it was a matter of principle, and Mummy said it was a matter of football, and Daddy proved it wasn't a matter of football by saying all right, he'd go, but only under some sort of umbrella called protest. And so on Saturday Jeremy James was suddenly face to face with a Mummy and Daddy who really didn't look like Mummy and Daddy at all. Mummy had on a black hat and a black dress and black stockings and black shoes, and Jeremy James asked her if she was going to sweep chimneys and Mummy said no she wasn't, and Daddy laughed. As for Daddy, he was wearing a dark grey suit, a black tie, and shoes that shone like glass.

'Is that really you, Daddy?' asked Jeremy James, and Daddy said he didn't think it was, and Mummy laughed. Then Mummy said they shouldn't be making jokes on a day like today, and Daddy said today was as good as any other day. Then Mummy dressed Jeremy James up in a smart grey suit he didn't even know he had, and off they drove to the funeral.

'You might have cleaned the car,' said Mummy.

'Weren't enough teardrops in the bucket,' said Daddy.

There were a few teardrops at the funeral, though.

Melissa, Aunt Janet's little girl, kept stamping her foot and saying she wanted her dolly, and Aunt Janet gave her a smack on her bottom which brought forth a whole flood of tears, but no dolly. Otherwise it was a very dull funeral, and the man who stood near the hole in the ground reading bits out of a book had the sort of voice that could put even dead people to sleep. The only interesting moment came when they lifted up a big wooden box and lowered it into the hole in the ground. It was a beautiful, shiny box, which looked very heavy and could have held at least a thousand bars of chocolate and two thousand soldiers.

'Daddy,' said Jeremy James, 'what's in the box?'

'Great-Aunt Maud,' said Daddy, and put his fingers on his lips.

'But what's she doing in there?' said Jeremy James.

'Being dead,' said Daddy.

'Well, what will she do when she wakes up?' said Jeremy James. 'Won't she bump her head?'

'She's not going to wake up,' said Daddy.

'Sh!' said Mummy.

'Why not?' said Jeremy James.

'Because she's dead,' said Daddy. 'Now keep quiet.'

'Well,' said Jeremy James, 'if she's not going to wake up, what does she need that box for?'

'That's enough, Jeremy James!' said Mummy, in her that's-enough voice.

Jeremy James would have liked to ask whether perhaps *he* could have the box since Great-Aunt Maud wouldn't be needing it any more, but when Mummy put on her that's-enough voice, that was enough.

After the funeral everyone drove to Uncle Jack and Aunt Janet's house, where they found lots and lots of lovely things to eat: sandwiches full of egg and cheese and lettuce and ham, cakes full of chocolate and cream and jam, biscuits, fruit, orange juice . . .

'Gosh!' said Jeremy James, 'this is a nice party!'

'Now you go and play with Melissa,' said Mummy.

'Oh I don't want to play with *her*,' said Jeremy James, 'I want to stay here by the table and eat all—'

'Off you go,' said Mummy.

But before Jeremy James could off-you-go even if he'd wanted to, which he didn't, he found himself face to waistcoat with a very, very, very old man whose tree-root hand came to rest upon his head, and whose watery blue eyes came to rest, one on his face and one round about his right shoulder. 'So this is your little boy, eh?' said a high creaky-door voice.

'That's right, Uncle Albert. This is Jeremy James. Jeremy James, this is your Great-Uncle Albert.'

'Hello,' said Jeremy James. 'You must be very old.'

'How old do you think I am?' said Great-Uncle Albert.

'Oh you must be at least a hundred,' said Jeremy James.

'Hmmph,' said Great-Uncle Albert, 'well I'm not that old, thank you very much.'

'How old *are* you then?' said Jeremy James.

'Jeremy James!' said Mummy.

'That's all right, my dear,' said Great-Uncle Albert, 'if the boy wants to know how old I am, I'll tell him how old I am, if I can remember how old I am. Let's see now, I was born in . . .' Great-Uncle Albert mumbled and muttered a sort of magic spell like 'O three seventy take away worple and add what you first thought of' and moved his tree-root down to Jeremy James's shoulder. 'Seventy-one!' he said, 'that's how old I am. Seventy-one!'

'Gosh!' said Jeremy James, 'you *are* old. You must be almost as old as Great-Aunt Maud.'

'Ah!' said Great-Uncle Albert. 'I couldn't be as old as her, because she was my mother.'

'You . . . you haven't got a mother, have you?' said Jeremy James, eyes as wide as jam tarts.

'Not now,' said Great-Uncle Albert.

'You look much too old to have a mother,' said Jeremy James, 'and that's a fact. Anyway, now that your mother's dead, she won't be needing her box any more, will she?'

'What box?' asked Great-Uncle Albert, proving yet again that grown-ups never even notice the most important things in life.

'The box they threw away this afternoon,' said Jeremy James. 'With her in it.'

'Jeremy James,' said Mummy, 'I think you should

go and play with Melissa now, dear. That's enough chatter for today.'

'But—'

'Off you go, dear.'

'I wanted—'

'And here's a nice piece of cream cake for you. Now go and play with Melissa.'

And Jeremy James found his mouth full to overflowing with cake, and he just couldn't say another word.

'What was that about a box?' he heard Great-Uncle Albert say.

'No idea,' said Mummy, 'you know how children talk.'

Jeremy James would have explained it to Great-Uncle Albert, but with a mouth full of cake, a chocolate biscuit in one hand and Mummy's hand in his other hand, he simply didn't have the chance to. Grown-ups are like that sometimes – when there's a really interesting subject to talk about, they tell you to keep quiet. But Mummy did give him a lot more cream cakes and chocolate biscuits, and he didn't have to play with Melissa after all because Melissa was sick and had to go up to her room, and when they were leaving, Uncle Jack pressed fifty pence into his hand and said, 'Here you are Jeremy James, buy yourself some sweets with that.' And when Great-Uncle Albert also gave him fifty pence (proving once more that uncles are full of good ideas), he knew for certain that this was the best party he'd ever been to.

'Mummy,' he said as Daddy angrily hooted the

crowds of people walking in the road outside the football stadium, 'I do like funerals. I hope someone else dies soon, so we can go to another one. Maybe Great-Uncle Albert'll die soon – he looks old enough.'

'That's not a very nice thing to say, dear,' said Mummy. 'You mustn't wish people would die.'

'What happened?' said Daddy through the window to a red-faced man with a moustache who was just overtaking the car.

'Lost,' said the red-faced man. 'Four-nil.'

'Hmmph,' said Daddy. 'Four-nil. They should shoot the lot of 'em!'

'That's not a very nice thing to say,' said Jeremy James – but Daddy didn't seem to hear, and Mummy was suddenly coughing into her handkerchief.

CHAPTER TWELVE

A Birth in the Family

Mummy wasn't well. Mummy hadn't been well for ages. Jeremy James thought she must have eaten an *enormous* number of sweets to be sick for such a long time, but Mummy only smiled and said it wasn't sweets at all. But Mummy's tummy was getting so big that Jeremy James didn't see what else it could possibly be, and he told Daddy what he thought, and Daddy only smiled and said the same as Mummy. And then Daddy looked at Mummy, and Mummy looked at Daddy, and they both smiled, and nodded, and then Mummy said to Jeremy James:

'Jeremy James, how would you like a little brother or sister?'

And Jeremy James thought for a minute or two, and said, 'I'd rather have some strawberries and ice cream.'

'Well if you're a very good boy,' said Mummy, 'we might let you have a brother *and* some strawberries and ice cream.'

This sounded rather interesting, and Jeremy James thought for another minute or two. 'Um,' he said – 'um' being his very own word to prepare the way for a request unlikely to be granted – 'um . . . can I have the strawberries and ice cream first, then?'

'You can have strawberries and ice cream for your tea today,' said Mummy, 'but you won't be getting your brother for quite a while yet.'

'Your sister,' said Daddy.

'Brother,' said Mummy.

And there really *were* strawberries and ice cream for tea, and Mummy felt much better, and Daddy kept jumping up and down to get things for Mummy, and Jeremy James kept jumping up and down to get things for Jeremy James, and it was a very jolly tea.

'Jeremy James,' said Daddy, 'which would you prefer, a brother or a sister?'

'A brother,' said Jeremy James. 'Because brothers are boys, and I'm a boy, and boys are best 'cos girls are silly.'

'Bad luck,' said Daddy, 'because it's a little girl called Jennifer, and that's a fact.'

'It's a little boy called Christopher,' said Mummy.

'Maybe the lady in the baby shop'll tell you,' said Jeremy James, though he wasn't too hopeful about that, as people in shops don't usually tell you very much, except to mind where you're going, or to take your hands off the clothes/toys/chocolate biscuits.

Mummy suddenly said 'Ow!' and put her hand on her tummy.

'What is it, dear?' asked Daddy, and did a cow-jumping-over-the-moon leap round the table.

'He kicked me!' said Mummy.

'She kicked you?' asked Daddy.

'He did,' said Mummy.

'Did she?' asked Daddy.

'Yes,' said Mummy.

And Jeremy James said nothing, because he was wondering just how Mummy could have been kicked when there was nobody in sight who might have kicked her. He and Daddy had certainly been over on the other side of the table, a quick look proved that there was nobody else *under* the table, and Jeremy James knew for a fact that there was nobody else in the room. Mummy really *was* ill.

'Come here, Jeremy James,' said Mummy. 'Come quickly.'

Jeremy James came sort of slowly-quickly to Mummy, making quite sure on his way that there definitely wasn't anybody within kicking distance.

Mummy took hold of his hand and placed it on her tummy.

'Feel that,' she said.

And then a very strange thing happened. From under Mummy's dress something jumped up against Jeremy James's hand, and it was just like a little kick.

'Did you feel it?' said Mummy.

And Jeremy James looked at her, wide-eyed . . . and felt another leapy-kicky-hiccuppy sort of jerk against his hand. 'That's your little brother,' said Mummy. 'He's inside there, having a good kick.'

'But Mummy,' said Jeremy James, 'what's he doing under your dress?'

'He's not under my dress,' said Mummy. 'He's . . . he's . . . well, you explain it to him, dear.'

'No, you explain it,' said Daddy.

'You explain it,' said Mummy. 'You're better at these things than I am.'

'What things?' asked Daddy.

'These things,' said Mummy. 'Things that need to be explained.'

Then Daddy explained to Jeremy James – while Mummy explained to Daddy – how babies grew inside their Mummy's tummy until they were big enough to come out . . . like an egg in a chicken . . . no, not quite like Number Two . . . well sort of . . . no, like an egg in a chicken but we'll get you a book when you're a bit older and that'll explain it much better . . .

'Well I don't remember being inside Mummy's tummy,' said Jeremy James.

'You were rather young at the time,' said Daddy.

'I'm too big to go inside Mummy's tummy,' said Jeremy James.

'You are now,' said Daddy, 'but you were small enough then.'

'Well, how do they get out?' said Jeremy James.

'We should never have started this,' said Daddy.

'Go on, tell him,' said Mummy. 'I'll clear the table.'

'No, you tell him, and I'll clear the table,' said Daddy.

'Well when they're ready,' said Mummy, 'they come out through a hole, that's all. And the doctor comes and helps them out.'

'So how do they get in?' asked Jeremy James.

'They just grow in there,' said Mummy. 'And when they're big enough they come out. And you'll see, when Christopher comes out, Mummy's tummy will go quite flat again.'

'*Quite* flat?' said Daddy.

'Fairly flat,' said Mummy.

'Well I don't remember being inside,' said Jeremy James, 'and I don't remember coming out either.'

'Well you *were* inside,' said Daddy, 'and you did come out, and that's enough!'

It was usually Mummy who said 'That's enough', but Daddy's voice was just like Mummy's this time, and Jeremy James decided that Daddy's 'That's enough' meant the same as Mummy's, though he would really have liked to find out a bit more about this funny grown-up way of getting babies in and out.

And so Jeremy James waited, and every tea-time he watched Mummy's tummy to see if a little boy would pop out of a hole and Mummy's tummy would go flat again, and Mummy kept saying 'Soon!' and Daddy kept saying 'Hmmph!' – and it was all very puzzling. Jeremy James still thought it would be much simpler if they went and bought their baby at the baby shop. There at least they'd be able to *see* whether it was a Christopher or a Jennifer, instead of feeling Mummy's tummy and trying to guess whether it was a boy-kick or a girl-kick. Grown-ups always make simple things complicated.

Jeremy James never did see any babies come out of Mummy's tummy. He just woke up one bright sun-beamy morning and heard all sorts of funny noises coming from Mummy and Daddy's bedroom. When he peeped in, he saw his old crib standing in the corner, and Daddy was standing next to it, rocking it backwards and forwards. There was a loud squeaky-squawky-squealy-squally noise coming from it, and Daddy was saying, 'Ssshhh now, ssshhh now, do as Daddy tells you!' in the sort of voice he sometimes used when he was mending things like the bathroom lock. But the squeaky-squawky-squealy-squally noise just got louder and louder, until Daddy stopped rocking the crib and said, 'All right, make as much noise as you blooming well like,' and then the noise stopped and the whole room was quiet, except for a

soft Little Bo-Peep sound from Mummy's bed, which meant that Mummy must be fast asleep.

Then Daddy caught sight of Jeremy James, and waved him in.

'Hey,' said Daddy, ever so quietly, 'come and look at Jennifer! But don't wake her!'

And Jeremy James tiptoed over to the corner, held Daddy's hand, and looked into the crib.

'But . . . but which of them,' asked Jeremy James, 'is Jennifer?'

'That one,' said Daddy, 'and that one's Christopher. Or is that one Christopher and that one Jennifer? No, Jennifer's the one with the pink, and Christopher's the one with the blue.'

'Why have we got *two* babies?' asked Jeremy James.

'Ah . . . um . . . well, it's all a matter of semantics, or something like that,' said Daddy.

'Oh,' said Jeremy James. 'Well did they both come out of Mummy's tummy?'

'Yes,' said Daddy.

'Were they both in there together?' asked Jeremy James.

'Yes,' said Daddy.

'And are we keeping them both?' asked Jeremy James.

'Yes,' said Daddy.

Jeremy James looked down at his brother and sister, and up at his Daddy, and across at his Mummy, and he thought for a very long time.

'Daddy,' he said at last, 'if Mummy had room in

her tummy for *two* babies, and I was once a baby in Mummy's tummy, where's the *other* baby that I was in Mummy's tummy with?'

'You do like asking questions, don't you?' said Daddy, and looked across at Mummy, but she was still sleeping. 'Well there wasn't another one,' said Daddy. 'You were all alone. Most babies are all alone, but Christopher and Jennifer are . . . well . . . they're twins . . . they're what we call something special.'

'What does "special" mean, Daddy?' asked Jeremy James.

'Well, if something is special,' said Daddy, 'it means there's nothing else like it. For instance, you're the only Jeremy James we've got, so you're special.'

'Are you special, too?' asked Jeremy James.

'Yes,' said Daddy. 'And so is Mummy. And so are Christopher and Jennifer.'

'Oh, they can't be special,' said Jeremy James, 'because there's two of them.'

'Well,' said Daddy, 'do you know any other babies quite like Christopher and Jennifer?'

'No-o,' said Jeremy James.

'Then that makes them special, too, doesn't it?' said Daddy.

And the more Jeremy James looked at his new brother and sister, the more special they really seemed to be. You certainly wouldn't be able to buy anything like them at the baby shop, and that was a fact.

Never Say Moo to a Bull

For Lisbeth,
with love

Contents

CHAPTER ONE

Daddy's New Car

Daddy had bought a new car. It was not a *new* new car, but a second-hand new car – in fact, an old second-hand new car. But although it was old, it was not as old as Daddy's old car, which had been very old indeed, and had been sat on by an elephant. Cars are not really designed to be sat on by elephants, and Daddy's old car had not been designed to be sat on by anything. Mummy said it was more of an ornament than a car, because it spent most of its time standing very still, either in the street outside or in the repair shop. When it did move, it was usually on the end of a rope, being pulled along by the van from the repair shop. Anyway, when the twins were born it was obvious that the family were going to need a bigger car (not to mention a car that could move), and so Daddy sold the old old car and bought the new old car.

It was a moment of great excitement when Daddy pulled up outside the house in a long blue limousine that shone like a new pair of shoes. He gave a toot on the hooter (which sounded much grander than

the honk of the old car), and Mummy and Jeremy James rushed out of the house to inspect the new arrival, while the twins were left in their cots to inspect the ceiling or each other.

'It's lovely,' said Mummy. 'It looks almost new!'

'Only done forty thousand miles,' said Daddy.

'That sounds a lot to me,' said Mummy.

'Not for a car,' said Daddy.

'How much did our old one do, Daddy?' asked Jeremy James.

'Never more than two yards at a time,' said Daddy. 'Come on, get the twins and we'll go for a run.'

Jeremy James wondered why they should go running when they'd just got a new car, but as they'd often gone walking when they'd had the old car, he assumed this was just the way grown-ups did things. In any case he had no time to ask as Mummy whisked him back into the house to get his coat on, and then went upstairs with Daddy to get Christopher and Jennifer ready.

'Let's go out into the country,' said Mummy.

'Or I could take her on the motorway,' said Daddy. 'Get up a bit of speed.'

'The country would be nicer,' said Mummy. 'And we can stop off somewhere for tea.'

Jeremy James pricked up his ears. He liked stopping off somewhere for tea. Platefuls of strawberries hovered before his eyes . . .

'Can I have cream on them?' he asked.

'Cream on what?' asked Mummy.

'On my strawberries,' said Jeremy James.

'You don't get strawberries at this time of the year,' said Mummy. 'You get hot buttered scones and toast and cakes.'

'And strawberry jam,' said Jeremy James.

'And strawberry jam if you like,' said Mummy.

'With cream on it,' said Jeremy James.

Mummy had changed Jennifer's nappy, and had wrapped her up in a clean dress and a woolly coat, and Jennifer was laughing happily. Daddy had just stabbed himself with the safety pin on Christopher's dirty nappy, and was sucking his injured thumb while Christopher was crying.

'I'll do him,' said Mummy. 'You hold Jennifer.'

111

'I'd better just get some plaster on this,' said Daddy.

Eventually both twins were ready, Christopher stopped crying, Daddy's thumb was plastered, the pram had been taken apart, both parts had been loaded into the back of the new car with the twins lying cosily in the top part, and Mummy and Daddy and Jeremy James were all strapped into their seats.

'Here we go, then,' said Daddy. 'Next stop Monte Carlo.'

Daddy turned a key, and there was a loud whirring sound. Daddy stopped turning the key, and the loud whirring sound stopped, too. Then Daddy turned the key again, and there was a loud whirring sound again. Daddy stopped turning, and everything was very quiet.

'Just . . . um . . . got cold . . .' said Daddy, and turned the key again. There was the same whirring sound, followed by the same silence.

'Could be flooded,' said Daddy. 'Unless it's over-heated. I'll take a look.'

He pulled a lever, unstrapped himself and got out. He went to the front of the car and then disappeared from view behind the raised bonnet.

'It sounded a bit like our old car, didn't it, Mummy?' said Jeremy James.

'Yes,' said Mummy. 'And it seems to go like our old car, too.'

Daddy came back.

'Can't see anything,' he said. 'I'll just give it another try.'

He sat in his seat and turned the key. There was a loud whirring sound, followed by a loud silence.

'Perhaps you'd better give them a ring,' said Mummy.

'Hmmmph!' said Daddy. 'I'll have another look.' And he got out again and disappeared again and came back again and sat down again. 'It's a lovely clean engine,' he said. 'Lovely, clean, and dead.'

'Why don't you give them a ring?' said Mummy.

'One more try,' said Daddy. 'If I can just take it by surprise.' He put his fingers round the key, looked out of the window, and then suddenly jerked his hand. There was a loud whirring sound. Daddy kept his hand turned, and the whirring sound gradually slowed till it became more of a wheezing than a whirring. Daddy relaxed his hand. There was silence.

'Perhaps I'd better give them a ring,' he said.

From the back of the car came a howl that was even louder than the loud whirring sound had been. Jennifer had kicked Christopher, and Christopher was much easier to start than Daddy's car. Even though Jennifer had only kicked him once, his howl motor was running at full speed.

'I'll get them back inside,' said Mummy, 'while you go to the phone box. Do you want to stay in the car, Jeremy James?'

'Oh, yes please,' said Jeremy James.

'Right. Daddy'll be back in a minute.'

Mummy and Daddy took a giggling Jennifer and a wailing Christopher into the house, then Daddy set off down the road to the phone box. Jeremy

James sat quietly in his seat, gazing at the starter key, the control panel and, above all, the steering wheel of Daddy's car. How he would love to sit at the steering wheel, and swing it round, and swing it back again. And how he would love to pull the levers and press the switches and flash and hoot and brrm brrm and eeek round corners.

With a tug and a squeeze and a wriggle, Jeremy James escaped from his straps and dived head first into Daddy's seat. Another little wriggle put him in just the right position, his nose level with the middle of the steering wheel. Jeremy James grasped the steering wheel firmly in both hands. 'Brrm brrm,' he said, and swung the car screeching round the bend, hot on the tail of a gang of escaped bandits. 'Eeow!' said Jeremy James, and 'Eerrk!' and 'Brrm brrm brrm!'

Then he jerked at the lever in the floor, just as he had seen Daddy do in the old car, and it clicked into a new position.

'Oh!' said Jeremy James. 'I hope I haven't broken it!'

He waggled the lever around, but it didn't seem to be broken. It was just a little loose.

'Maybe that's how it *ought* to be,' said Jeremy James. 'Maybe that's what was wrong – Daddy had it in the wrong place!'

Jeremy James did some hard thinking. If Daddy *had* had it in the wrong place, and it was now in the right place, the car should go. And wouldn't Mummy and Daddy be pleased if the car went. They would be so pleased that they would give Jeremy

James hundreds of scones and thousands of cakes and millions of kisses. He would be a hero. If the car went. Jeremy James looked hard at the starter key. Jeremy James turned the starter key. But nothing happened. There was not even a whirring sound.

Jeremy James did some more hard thinking. Perhaps the car *shouldn't* make a whirring sound. Perhaps silence was what you *ought* to hear when you turned the key, and the loud whirring sound had been a sign that the lever in the floor was in the wrong position, only Daddy hadn't known that because, after all, this was a new car. Perhaps the car was all ready to go now the lever was in the right position.

Jeremy James tried to remember what Daddy used to do with the old car when it was ready to go. Wasn't there another lever Daddy used to pull?

Jeremy James looked for another lever. And sure enough, right behind the first lever he had pulled there was a second lever, and it had a button in it. Jeremy James smiled to himself, pressed the button, and gently lowered the second lever to the floor.

There was a creak, a little jerk, and . . . the car . . . was it? . . . yes, the car was moving! He'd done it! Oh, wouldn't Mummy and Daddy be pleased! Jeremy James lifted himself up in the seat so that he could look out of the window, and there was no doubt about it, the houses on the other side of the street were slowly slipping by in the opposite direction. In fact, they were slipping by a little faster now. In fact, even as he looked, they seemed to be gather-

ing speed. Jeremy James stopped smiling, and his heart began to pound. He hadn't meant to go as fast as this! He took hold of the steering wheel, but then he couldn't see out of the window any more, and so he just swung the steering wheel from side to side and wished he hadn't mended Daddy's car after all.

There was a loud thump and a tinkle of broken glass, and the car suddenly stopped. It stopped so suddenly that Jeremy James was thrown forward and bumped his nose hard on the middle of the steering wheel. The thump and the bump brought tears into and out of Jeremy James's eyes, and he sat at the steering wheel howling louder than the loud whirring noise and Christopher's wail put together. Then the car door opened, and there was Daddy lifting him out and holding him very tightly. And Mummy came running a moment later, and took him from Daddy, and asked if her little darling was all right, and Daddy said her little darling was all right, but his new car jolly well wasn't. Then Mummy said they shouldn't have left Jeremy James alone in the car, and Daddy said Jeremy James should have kept his hands off Daddy's new car, and Jeremy James howled very loudly because that seemed the safest thing to do.

There were soon quite a lot of people standing round Daddy's new car. Jeremy James heard their voices through Mummy's shoulder and they were saying things like 'How did it happen?' and 'Could have been killed!' and 'Who's going to pay for my garden wall?' and 'Don't worry, Mr Johnson, I'll see to everything, I'm ever so sorry ...' The last one was definitely Daddy's voice. Then Mummy carried Jeremy James away, and he risked a little peep over the top of her shoulder. Daddy's new car was right across the pavement, with its front all squashed up against a wall, and Daddy was talking to a red-faced man with a bristling moustache, and there was a policeman coming up the road towards them. Jeremy James hid his face again and let out a few more loud sobs.

'It's all right,' said Mummy, giving him an extra pat and a squeeze, 'don't cry. It's all right.'

Then she carried him into the house and gave him a big piece of chocolate, which helped to dry his eyes and silence his sobs. Chocolate was a medicine Jeremy James always responded to very quickly.

A little while later, Mummy called him to come and look out of the window, and she picked him up again so that he could get a good view. The van from the repair shop was just going by, and it was followed by a long rope, and on the end of the rope was Daddy's new car, looking very crumpled. At the steering wheel of Daddy's new car was Daddy, and he was looking rather crumpled, too.

'Oh Mummy,' said Jeremy James, 'it looks just like the old car now.'

'Hmmmph!' said Mummy, and held him very tight.

CHAPTER TWO

How to Get Rich

'How do you make money?' asked Jeremy James one morning at breakfast.

'No idea,' said Daddy. 'But if you ever find out, let me know.'

'You have to work for it,' said Mummy. 'You work, and then people pay you.'

'What sort of work?' asked Jeremy James.

'All sorts,' said Mummy. 'Different people do different work.'

'Well, what sort of work could I do to get some money?' asked Jeremy James.

'What do *you* need money for?' asked Mummy.

'Spending,' said Jeremy James.

'Spending on what?' asked Mummy.

Why was it that grown-ups never answered questions? You could ask them about anything, but they would never tell you what you wanted to know. Only yesterday he'd asked Mummy why the man they'd just walked past had one leg instead of two, and Mummy had said 'Sh!' to him as if he'd said something rude. 'I only want to know what's happened to his other leg,' Jeremy James had said, but Mummy had shushed him again with a threatening look. And the day before that, when he'd watched Mummy bathing the twins and had asked why Jennifer hadn't got something he and Christopher *had* got, all he received was a 'Hmmmph!' instead of an answer. You never get answers from grown-ups. Just 'sh', 'hmmph', or questions about why you were asking questions.

'Toys,' said Jeremy James. 'So that I can buy more toys.' He would have said sweets, but he knew what Mummy would say about more sweets.

'Haven't you got enough toys?' asked Mummy.

'Well I haven't got a tricycle with a saddlebag,' said Jeremy James. 'So how can I get money for a tricycle with a saddlebag?'

'I haven't got a tricycle with a saddlebag either,' said Daddy. 'It seems to be a common weakness in the family.'

Daddy tended not to say 'sh' or 'hmmmph' or ask questions; he just said things that had nothing to do with what you were asking.

'Well, what work can I do?' asked Jeremy James, who could be very determined when there was something to be determined about.

'Let's have a look in the paper,' said Daddy. 'See if we can find something suitable.'

And Daddy spread the paper out at the page where it said 'Jobs Vacant'.

'Now then,' he said. 'How about "long-distance lorry-driver"? No, not after your efforts at short-

distance car-driving. "Cook required part-time at nursing home." What's your cooking like, Jeremy James?'

'I'm good at strawberries and ice cream,' said Jeremy James.

'But you'd never leave any for the patients,' said Daddy.

'That's true,' said Jeremy James. 'But I'd like that sort of work.'

'I expect you would,' said Daddy. 'It's the kind of job you can grow fat on. How about being a coalman?'

'Too dirty,' said Jeremy James.

'A street cleaner, then?' said Daddy.

'I don't like cleaning,' said Jeremy James.

121

'Ah,' said Daddy. 'So it's got to be something that won't make you dirty and won't make you clean.'

'And they must pay me lots of money,' said Jeremy James.

'Nothing like that here, I'm afraid,' said Daddy, closing the paper. 'Fairy godmothers don't advertise in our paper.'

Mummy and Daddy smiled at each other, but Jeremy James didn't think it was funny. Sweets (and toys and tricycles with saddlebags) cost money, and if you wanted money you had to work, and if you couldn't work, you couldn't have money, and without money you couldn't have sweets (or toys or tricycles with saddlebags). And that wasn't at all funny. Jeremy James frowned. And behind his frown there began to stir a vague memory from the distant past. It had been at least two days ago. He had gone round the corner with Mummy to the greengrocer's shop, and in the greengrocer's window had been a large notice which Mummy had helped him to read. 'Bright Lad Wanted' – that's what the notice had said. Jeremy James thought hard for a moment.

'Mummy,' said Jeremy James. 'Am I bright?'

'As bright as a button,' said Mummy.

Jeremy James thought hard for another moment.

'Daddy,' said Jeremy James. 'How much do bright lads get paid?'

'Depends what they're doing,' said Daddy.

'Sort of . . . well . . . greengrocing?' said Jeremy James.

122

'No idea,' said Daddy. 'I expect they get the union rates for bright greengrocing lads.'

'What's union rates?' asked Jeremy James.

'That's what you'll get paid when you get the job,' said Daddy.

Jeremy James did some more hard thinking. The problem was not what to do, but how to get permission to do it. He looked at Mummy, and he looked at Daddy, and he looked at the table, and he took a deep breath and said: 'Can I just go round the corner to the . . . um . . . sweetshop?'

To his surprise, Mummy gave him permission without asking a single question.

'Good luck!' said Daddy, as Jeremy James left the house.

'But don't go into the road,' said Mummy, 'and come straight home afterwards.'

Jeremy James walked proudly and brightly up the street and round the corner to the greengrocer's shop. The notice was still in the window. Jeremy James puffed out his chest, and marched in.

'And what can we do for you?' asked a thin man in a brown coat, with a face like a wizened apple.

'I'm a bright lad,' said Jeremy James.

'Aha!' said the wizened apple. 'I can see that. But what can I do for you?'

'Well, I've come for the job,' said Jeremy James. 'So that I can get enough money for a tricycle with a saddlebag. And you should pay me onion rates.'

'Onion rates, eh?' said the man in the brown coat. 'What's your name, then, sonny?'

'Jeremy James,' said Jeremy James.

'That's a smart-sounding name all right,' said the man in the brown coat. 'But to tell you the truth, Jeremy James, we were really looking for someone a little older and a little bigger.'

'I'll be getting bigger,' said Jeremy James. 'I've grown quite a lot since last week.'

'Oh you'll be growing fast, I'm sure,' said the man. 'You'll be growing at onion rates, won't you? But you see, we need someone to carry big loads of fruit and vegetables around. And he'd have to be able to carry them on a bicycle to the houses around here.'

'Well I could put them in my saddlebag,' said Jeremy James. 'When I've got a saddlebag.'

'And when you've got a tricycle,' said the man.

'Yes,' said Jeremy James.

'No, I don't think that would work,' said the man. 'Because there's an awful lot to carry.'

'I'll get a *big* saddlebag,' said Jeremy James.

'In any case,' said the man, 'you couldn't do the job till you had your tricycle. And you can't have your tricycle till you've done the job. It's what's called a vicious circle. Or cycle.'

Jeremy James's head dropped down on his chest like a cabbage too heavy for its stalk.

'I'll tell you what,' said the man. 'You try and grow nice and quickly, and when you're as tall as my shoulder, come back and I'll give you the job.'

'I'll never be as tall as your shoulder,' said Jeremy James.

'If you eat plenty of fresh fruit and vegetables,' said the man, 'you'll be up past my shoulder in no time. And I'll start you off myself, how's that? Come here, Jeremy James. Now take this paper bag.'

Jeremy James took the large paper bag that the man held out to him.

'Now you go round my shop,' said the man, 'and fill that paper bag with anything you like.'

'Anything?' said Jeremy James.

'Anything,' said the man.

Jeremy James looked round the shop. Apples, oranges, pears, bananas ... potatoes, tomatoes, beans, carrots ...

'You haven't got any chocolate, have you?' asked Jeremy James.

'Afraid not,' said the man.

'Or any tins of mandarin oranges?' asked Jeremy James.

'No tins here,' said the man. 'Everything fresh as God made it.'

Jeremy James filled his bag until its sides were splitting and he needed both hands and both arms to hold it all together.

'Off you go, then, Jeremy James,' said the man, 'and I'll see you when you're up to my shoulder.'

'All right,' said Jeremy James. 'I'll be back next week. Thank you very much for the bagful.'

When Mummy and Daddy saw the bag of fruit, their eyes opened as wide as apples.

'Where did that come from?' asked Mummy.

'I went for a job at the greengrocer's,' said Jeremy James.

'Did you get it?' asked Daddy.

'Well, not exactly,' said Jeremy James. 'He said I should come back next week when I'm as tall as his shoulder.'

'Ah,' said Daddy, 'and he gave you all this to help you grow.'

'Yes,' said Jeremy James. 'I'll be growing at onion rates.'

'Well, that is a lovely lot of fruit,' said Mummy, emptying the bag on to the table. 'Worth a small fortune.'

An idea came into Jeremy James's mind, and lit up his eyes from inside.

'Well, it is mine,' he said, 'but you can have it for nothing if you give me some money for it.'

Mummy looked at Daddy, and Daddy looked at Mummy.

'Fair enough,' said Daddy. 'If you want free fruit, you must pay for it.'

'How much are you asking?' said Mummy.

'It's worth a small fortune,' said Jeremy James. 'But I'd like enough to buy a tricycle with a saddlebag.'

'Oh,' said Mummy, 'now that would be a large fortune.'

'All right,' said Jeremy James. 'Enough for a box of liquorice allsorts.'

And to Jeremy James's surprise and delight, Mummy agreed. Ten minutes later Jeremy James was hurrying back up the road and round the corner to the sweetshop, and on his face was a smile as wide as a banana. It was the smile of a man who had done a good day's work.

CHAPTER THREE

The Christening

Christopher and Jennifer were to be christened. Jeremy James found the idea of christening a little difficult to understand. Mummy explained to him that the twins would be named and dipped in water, but Jeremy James pointed out that they already had names and that Mummy dipped them in water every day, so why did they have to go to church to be given names they already had and a bath which they didn't need? Then Mummy said Jesus wanted little children to be christened, but Jeremy James reckoned Jesus couldn't have known the twins had already been given their names and their bath. Then Mummy said Jeremy James was too young to understand but he could look forward to the party afterwards, and Jeremy James decided that if there was going to be a party afterwards, maybe christenings were a good thing after all and Jesus knew what he was doing.

There were not many people in the church, which seemed all dusty and hollow, and the people who *were* there talked in very quiet voices, as if they were afraid to wake somebody up.

129

'Mummy,' said Jeremy James in a loud voice that echoed round the walls of the church, 'why is everybody whispering?'

One or two heads turned in Jeremy James's direction and Mummy's face went a little red.

'Because,' whispered Mummy, 'you're not supposed to talk loudly in church.'

Mummy looked very smart in a blue suit with a flowery blue hat, and she was holding Christopher, who was wrapped up in a soft blue shawl. Christopher was peeping round him, and didn't seem to like what he saw. There was a slightly alarmed expression in his eyes, and his lips were turned down at both ends. Although the sun shone brightly outside the church, there was a distinct threat of showers inside.

Daddy also looked very smart in his grey suit with a neat grey and white tie. He was holding a pink-shawled Jennifer, who giggled loudly as Daddy tickled her under the chin. Daddy had to stop tickling her, because Jennifer didn't understand that you weren't supposed to make loud noises in church.

And between Mummy and Daddy stood Jeremy James, in a suit as grey as Daddy's, with his face scrubbed clean and his hair well brushed and parted. He gazed round the high, hollow church, and wondered why God chose to live in such a gloomy place. He reckoned God would be a lot happier if someone were to stick paper chains across His ceiling.

As Jeremy James gazed and pondered, the door

of the church opened and in came Uncle Jack, Aunt Janet, and Melissa, who was the same age as Jeremy James. Uncle Jack and Aunt Janet caught sight of Mummy and Daddy, and gave them a cheerful wave. Melissa caught sight of Jeremy James and stuck out her tongue. Jeremy James screwed up his face, put his thumb to his nose, and waggled his fingers. Just as he did so, the Reverend Cole hobbled up the aisle and drew level with Mummy.

'Ah, good morning!' said the Reverend Cole in a hollow creaky voice, and peered short-sightedly at Mummy. 'You must be . . . ah yes, of course . . . and this is . . .'

'Christopher,' said Mummy, 'and my husband's holding Jennifer.'

'That's right,' said the Reverend Cole, 'Christopher and Jennifer . . . I must remember that.' Then the Reverend Cole peered short-sightedly at Jeremy James. 'And what's this little girl's name?'

'Jeremy James,' said Jeremy James. 'But . . .'

'Jeremy James,' said the Reverend Cole, bending his tall thin body over like a hairpin, 'that's an unusual name for a little girl.'

'I'm a little boy,' said Jeremy James.

'Ah, that explains it,' said the Reverend Cole. 'Now when it's time, I want you and your family and friends to come to the back and gather round the font. All right? You can't miss it. So nice to see you. Christopher and Jennifer . . . two for the price of one, eh?'

And the Reverend Cole hobbled away to begin the service. The Reverend Cole always hobbled, because he was very old and his legs were very rubbery, but today his hobble was mixed with a wobble because yesterday, quite by accident, he had sat on a wasp and the wasp had stung him. The wasp, of course, had died, but the Reverend Cole had been left with a sore bottom.

When the service began, the Reverend Cole spoke out in a very loud voice, though Jeremy James wasn't sure what he was saying. Jeremy James whispered to Mummy that she should tell the man he wasn't supposed to talk loudly in church, but Mummy said 'Sh!', and just then everybody started singing at the tops of their voices: 'Blessed Jesus, here we stand.' One moment you had to be very quiet and the next moment you had to be very loud – that was typical grown-up topsy-turvy. 'Blessed Jesus, here we stand,' they sang, as if Jesus didn't know already.

At last, after more singing, talking, mumbling, and one long silence when everybody was supposed to close their eyes but Jeremy James didn't and nothing happened to him, the Reverend Cole eased himself out of the pulpit and trod painfully up the aisle.

As Mummy and Daddy were carrying the babies, they had to be very close to the Reverend Cole and the big stone saucer in which the twins were to take their bath. There was no room for Jeremy James as well, and so he found himself standing just behind the tall stooping figure of the Reverend Cole. On the other side of the Reverend Cole stood Uncle Jack and Aunt Janet, and behind them, exactly level with Jeremy James, was Cousin Melissa. She was wearing pigtails and a red and white spotted dress, and she was carrying a doll with pigtails and a red and white spotted dress, and she thought she looked pretty but Jeremy James didn't think she looked pretty. Jeremy James thought she looked ugly. And he thought her doll looked ugly, too. It was a job to decide which was uglier, Melissa or her doll. 'You both look ugly,' whispered Jeremy James to Melissa, and pulled the doll's pigtail.

'Stop it!' said Melissa, in a loud voice. Heads turned.

'Sh!' said Aunt Janet, with a frown.

'Jennifer, I baptize thee in the name of the Father and of the Son and of the Holy Spirit. Amen,' said the Reverend Cole, and bent over the font like a giraffe picking daisies. He sprinkled her with water, and she came up smiling.

'Aaaah!' said several voices at once, as the Reverend Cole handed her back to a proud Daddy.

'You're smelly,' whispered Jeremy James to Melissa.

'So are you,' whispered Melissa to Jeremy James.

'Not as smelly as you,' whispered Jeremy James to Melissa.

Mummy handed Christopher over to the Reverend Cole. He was scarcely halfway across when the thunderstorm broke. Tears rained from his eyes and a piercing howl gusted out of his wide-open mouth. A shudder ran through the assembly, and the Reverend Cole thought seriously of retirement.

'Your doll is as ugly and smelly as you are,' whispered Jeremy James to Melissa.

'I'm going to tell on you,' said Melissa to Jeremy James.

'Just like a girl,' said Jeremy James to Melissa, and this time he pulled one of Melissa's pigtails.

'You stop it!' cried Melissa, and gave Jeremy James a good hard push.

As Jeremy James had had to lean over to pull Melissa's pigtail, he was off balance when she pushed him. He staggered, and he would certainly have fallen if he hadn't managed to hold on to the nearest support. The nearest support was the Reverend Cole, and as the Reverend Cole was at that moment bending over the font to give Christopher his bath, Jeremy

James grasped the very part of the Reverend Cole on which the dead wasp had chosen to make its mark.

'Christopher, I baptize thee in the name of the Faaaaaaaaaah!' cried the Reverend Cole, and dropped the howling Christopher straight into the font. Mummy swiftly scooped her wet and wailing baby out of the water, the Reverend Cole stood trembling, with one hand clasped to his bottom and the other flapping uselessly in the air, Daddy gaped and Jennifer gurgled, and Jeremy James quickly squeezed in between Mummy and Daddy and stood very still, gazing up at the font.

'Oh dear ... most unfortunate ... lively little fellow ...' said the Reverend Cole. 'Um ... perhaps you'd better hold him now ...'

By the time the Reverend Cole had finished the service, Christopher's squalls had died down into occasional sobs, though they did flare up again when the Reverend Cole muttered, 'There's a good boy,' and tried to pat him on the head. And by the time they all got home, he had fallen into a deep healing sleep, which Mummy piously thanked Heaven for.

The party was a great success. Jeremy James handed round platefuls of sandwiches and cakes and showed everyone how to eat them. Melissa was sick, and Uncle Jack and two other uncles each gave Jeremy James fifty pence on their way out. Jeremy James reckoned that Jesus really did know what he was doing when he invented christenings.

'Could have been quite nasty,' said Daddy, when

everyone had gone and they were left with nothing but memories and dirty dishes.

'What on earth made him shout like that?' said Mummy. 'And fancy dropping poor Christopher in the font!'

'He's obviously past it,' said Daddy. 'Should be made to lie down in green pastures if you ask me.'

'Anyway,' said Mummy, 'everything else went well. And I thought Jeremy James was a very good boy today.'

Daddy put his arm round his son. 'That's true,' he said. 'Never heard a word from him right through the service. There'll be a bonus on your pocket money this week, my boy.'

Jeremy James gave a big smile, and gazed innocently up at his proud Mummy and Daddy. The fact that grown-ups live in a topsy-turvy world can sometimes have its advantages.

CHAPTER FOUR

Timothy's Birthday Party

Timothy was the boy who lived in the big house next door. He was a year older than Jeremy James, and he knew everything there was to know, and he had everything there was to have. Timothy went to school, though Jeremy James wasn't quite sure whether Timothy went there as a pupil or as a teacher, since he knew such a lot. And although on every day of the year Timothy was more important than anybody else, today he was doubly more important, because today was his birthday. He had long ago invited all his friends to the best birthday party they would ever be lucky enough to attend, and Jeremy James was one of the chosen few.

'Ding-dong!' said the front doorbell of Timothy's house, and a moment later the door had opened and there stood Timothy's mummy.

'Hello, Mrs Smyth-Forcitick,' said Jeremy James. (The name was Smyth-Fortescue, but Jeremy James couldn't quite get his tongue in the right position.)

'Hello, Jeremy James,' said Mrs Smyth-Fortescue.

'Hello, Jeremy James.

'That's right. Do come in, Jeremy.'

And a moment later, Jeremy James was face to face with the great hero himself.

'Happy birthday, Tim,' said Jeremy James, handing over a large box-shaped parcel wrapped in thick brown paper and tied up with string. It was a very exciting parcel, and Jeremy James knew just what was inside it and he wished it was for him and not for Timothy.

Timothy pulled the string apart and tore open the brown paper (which he simply dropped on the floor and left – perhaps as a special treat for his Mummy). Inside was a box, and inside the box was a tank. It was a brown and green tank with a gun that could swivel and fire matches, and it had an engine of its own which meant it could roll along the carpet all by itself, and as it rolled it sparked and made a loud grinding noise, just like a real tank. Jeremy James had seen it working in the shop when he and Mummy had bought it, and he'd seen it again in the living room when Daddy had tested it (for three-quarters of an hour), and Timothy was very lucky to get a tank like that because a tank like that was the best present anybody could ever have.

'Oh yes, I've got one like this already,' said Timothy. 'Only the one I've got is bigger.'

A little light of hope shone through Jeremy James's eyes: 'Don't you want it, then?' he asked.

'Oh yes, I'll take it,' said Timothy. 'I don't mind having two.'

Out went the little light of hope.

When Timothy had shown off all his presents to all his friends, and had made it clear to them that he had more presents and better presents than they were ever likely to get, and they were very lucky to have a friend like him, all the boys went out into the Smyth-Fortescues' huge garden. There they whooped and warbled, hid and sought, shot and scalped, swung and slid, and machine-gunned one another down until teatime. Tea was a rich feast of sandwiches, crisps, cakes, jelly, ice cream and fizzy drinks. Jeremy James's arms, hands and jaws worked almost continuously as he reached, grabbed and chewed, and with all the other boys doing the same, it wasn't long before the dining table was as bare as old Mother Hubbard's cupboard.

'Finished, everybody?' asked Mrs Smyth-Fortescue.

'Is there any more?' asked Timothy.

'No, dear.'

'Then I suppose we've finished,' said Timothy, with a glance at the tableful of bare plates.

'Well, I'll just clear the table,' said Mrs Smyth-Fortescue, 'then we can play some nice games, hm?'

While she was clearing the table, Mr Smyth-Fortescue came home from work. He had ginger hair and freckles just like Timothy, and he poked them round the door.

'Are you all enjoying yourselves?' he asked.

Nobody took the slightest notice of him, so he went out and wasn't seen again.

'Games now, children!' said Mrs Smyth-Fortescue. 'And there are lovely prizes for the winners.'

'It's bars of chocolate,' said Timothy. 'And I'm going to win them all.'

'I hope I can win one,' said Jeremy James as the prize bars emerged from the sideboard.

'No, you're not allowed,' said Timothy, ' 'cos it's *my* birthday.'

'Not much fun if we can't win,' said Richard, a fat boy with a round red face.

'I wouldn't win anyway,' said Trevor, a tiny boy who'd already cried twice in the garden.

'Hunt the thimble!' cried Mrs Smyth-Fortescue. 'Everybody leave the room while I hide it!'

And everybody left the room, though Richard and Trevor tried to leave it together, which resulted in a rather squashed Trevor having his third cry of the day.

'Ready!' called Mrs Smyth-Fortescue, and everybody re-entered the room, with Timothy pushing through the door first and Trevor and Jeremy James waiting until it was safe, which meant until Richard had gone in.

'Who's warmest, Mummy?' asked Timothy.

'Jeremy,' said Mrs Smyth-Fortescue.

And as Jeremy James turned round to tell her his name was Jeremy *James*, there was a blur of ginger, and Jeremy James found himself flat on his back next to the piano.

'Got it!' shouted Timothy. 'I got it! Here it is! I got it!'

'Oh well done, dear!' said Mrs Smyth-Fortescue. 'But try not to knock Jeremy down next time.'

Jeremy James rose to his feet and watched Timothy collect his bar of chocolate.

'If he hadn't gone and knocked me over, I'd have had that chocolate,' he said to little Trevor. 'It's not fair.'

'Now we're going to stick the tail on the donkey,' said Mrs Smyth-Fortescue.

'I'll go last,' said Timothy.

'Right, now who's going first?' asked Mrs Smyth-Fortescue. 'Come along, Jeremy.'

'Jeremy *James*,' said Jeremy James.

'That's right,' said Mrs Smyth-Fortescue, tying the blindfold over his eyes and spinning him round

twice. 'There you are, Jeremy. Now try and put the tail on the donkey.'

There were hoots of laughter as Jeremy James proceeded to stick the tail on the donkey's nose. And the hoots of laughter continued as each boy in turn stabbed the donkey where it shouldn't have been stabbed. Trevor was the nearest – sticking it on the donkey's back leg – until Timothy received the blindfold. He walked straight up to the wall, and without a moment's hesitation stuck the tail in exactly the right position.

'Oh well done, dear!' cried Mrs Smyth-Fortescue, and Timothy collected his second bar of chocolate.

'The blindfold wasn't on properly,' said fat Richard quietly.

'I was winning that,' said little Trevor sadly.

'None of us'll win anything,' said Jeremy James miserably.

And as the afternoon went on, it looked as though he was going to be right. Timothy won all the memory games and all the guessing games, never making a single mistake; and when they played Murder in the Dark, Timothy insisted on being the murderer, which meant there were no prizes anyway because if you knew who the murderer was, there was no game left. Jeremy James wished he could have been the murderer, because he would jolly well have murdered Timothy, and he would *really* have murdered Timothy, and no one would have cried a tear, except perhaps Mrs Smyth-Fortisoup.

Timothy also won Musical Chairs. He shouldn't have won it, because when he and a boy called Rodney were the last ones left, Timothy sat down *before* the music stopped, but his Mummy *saw* that he'd sat down and *then* she stopped the music. *Everybody* said that was unfair, but Timothy said it was *his* party, and his Mummy said it was his birthday and they should be nice to him and it had been such a lovely party and they shouldn't quarrel, and Timothy said if they didn't let him win they could jolly well go home, and his Mummy said, 'There, there, darling,' and gave him an extra bar of chocolate to comfort him, and then announced that the prize for the last game would be three bars of chocolate, which cheered everybody up.

'I'm going to win it,' said Timothy, which cheered everybody down.

The game was Musical Statues. Mrs Smyth-Fortescue would play the piano, and when she stopped, everybody would stand still, but whoever moved *after* she had stopped would be out. The last one left would be the winner. As she started playing, all the boys started walking, and there were lots of determined faces moving round the room. But with each pause in the music, determination gave way to disappointment and more drooping figures sat down next to the wall. Finally, there were just three boys left: Timothy, Trevor, and Jeremy James (though twice Timothy had moved but he said he hadn't and his Mummy didn't think he had either). Round they went, to the merry tinkle of the piano, and Jeremy James could feel that Timothy was right behind him. He walked faster, but Timothy was still there. He walked slower, and . . . the piano stopped. Bump! Jeremy James went flying, while Timothy, who had walked straight into him, stood as stiff as a candle on a birthday cake.

'Oh bad luck, Jeremy!' called Mrs Smyth-Fortescue.

'It wasn't bad luck,' said Jeremy James, 'he knocked me over.'

'*Very* bad luck,' said Mrs Smyth-Fortescue. 'On we go! I wonder who's going to win!'

'Hmmmph!' said Jeremy James, very loud, and slumped down on the floor next to fat Richard. 'It's obvious who's going to win. *He's* going to win. Because *she's* going to let him win.'

'It's a rotten party,' said Richard. 'I wish I hadn't come.'

There were more merry tinkles from the piano, and then the music stopped. But just as it stopped, Jeremy James noticed something, and what he noticed was to make the rotten party into a good party after all. He noticed that Trevor had stopped quite still on the far side of the room, and Timothy had stopped quite still on Jeremy James's side. But whereas Trevor was standing on the shiny wooden floor, Timothy was standing on the edge of a round woollen rug. And the round woollen rug reached just as far as where Jeremy James was sitting, and the edge of it was a mere inch away from his right hand. And Jeremy James's right hand took an immediate decision. It grasped the edge of the round woollen rug, and gave it a quick, hard jerk.

'He moved!' cried a dozen voices, and a dozen fingers pointed as Timothy wobbled, staggered, almost fell, and then righted himself and pretended nothing had happened.

'I didn't!' said Timothy.

'I'm afraid you did, dear,' said Mrs Smyth-Fortescue.

'We all saw you,' said Jeremy James.

'It wasn't me,' said Timothy, 'it was the floor. The floor moved.'

146

'No, the floor couldn't have moved, dear,' said Mrs Smyth-Fortescue.

'It did, it did!' said Timothy. 'The floor moved! I felt it! I know what it was! It was the rug!'

Jeremy James frowned.

'Richard pulled the rug!'

Jeremy James stopped frowning.

'It was Richard pulling the rug! It was, Mummy! Ask him! Richard pulled the rug, Mummy!'

'Now then, Richard,' said Mrs Smyth-Fortescue, 'is that true? Did you pull the rug, dear!'

'No I didn't,' said Richard.

'He did!' said Timothy.

'I didn't!' said Richard.

'Jeremy,' said Mrs Smyth-Fortescue, 'did you see Richard pull the rug?'

'No, Mrs Smyth-Fortisook,' said Jeremy James, 'he couldn't have done 'cos I'm sitting next to him and I'd have seen him. He didn't pull it. Definitely!'

'Very well,' said Mrs Smyth-Fortescue. 'Here you are, Trevor. Come and collect your prize.'

And a dozen voices let out a loud cheer as Trevor collected his three bars of chocolate.

'It's not fair!' wailed Timothy. 'They cheated! It's not fair!'

'Time for everybody to go home now!' said Mrs Smyth-Fortescue.

Timothy stamped his foot, stormed out of the room, up the stairs, and into his bedroom, slamming the door behind him.

Mrs Smyth-Fortescue was taking some of the children home by car, but Jeremy James, Trevor and Richard all lived nearby, so they left together.

'Thank you for the nice party, Mrs Smyth-Forkisuit,' said Jeremy James before they went.

'Glad you enjoyed it, Jeremy,' said Mrs Smyth-Fortescue, giving each of them a balloon and a piece of birthday cake.

'Jeremy *James*,' said Jeremy James.

'That's right,' said Mrs Smyth-Fortescue.

Jeremy James, Trevor and Richard walked together to Jeremy James's front gate. Trevor was loaded down with his balloon, his cake, and his three bars of chocolate, but he had a very important question to ask before they parted company.

'Richard,' he said, '*did* you pull the rug?'

'No,' said Richard, 'I didn't.'

'But I did,' said Jeremy James.

And as they all laughed, Trevor looked at his bars of chocolate, looked at Richard's face, looked at Jeremy James's face, and then looked at his chocolate again.

'Here,' he said. 'I think we *all* deserve a prize.' And he gave each of them a bar of chocolate.

'Was it a nice party, dear?' asked Mummy, opening the door for Jeremy James.

'Yes, thank you,' said Jeremy James. 'I won a bar of chocolate.'

'And what did you win that for?' asked Mummy.

CHAPTER FIVE

The Tooth Dragon

Jeremy James had toothache. It was a tooth over on the right-hand side of his mouth, and without a doubt it was his favourite chocolate-crunching, liquorice allsort-munching tooth. Mummy said it had probably been crunching too much chocolate and too many liquorice allsorts, and that was why it was hurting, but Jeremy James reckoned it was too many potatoes and too much cabbage that had done the damage. After all, it was his tooth, so he should know what was good and bad for it. But at the moment, he had to confess, the favourite tooth had as little enthusiasm for chocolate and liquorice allsorts as it had for potatoes and cabbage. It couldn't munch, and it couldn't crunch. All it could do was ache.

'Is it very bad?' asked Mummy at breakfast, as Jeremy James's teeth and tongue wrestled with a cornflake.

Jeremy James pulled a face like a crumpled chocolate wrapper. 'Very, very bad,' he said. Then he remembered something Daddy had said once, when

151

Mummy asked him how he was after he'd mistaken his thumb for the picture hook. 'It's agony,' said Jeremy James, 'blooming agony.'

'I'll ring Mr Pulham,' said Mummy.

'Who's Mr Pulham?' asked Daddy.

'The dentist!' said Mummy.

'Ah yes,' said Daddy. 'I believe he's of American extraction. What they call a Yank.'

Mummy and Daddy both laughed, but Jeremy James remained very serious, because toothache is no laughing matter.

'Will it hurt?' asked Jeremy James, as he and Mummy pushed the twins along in their pram.

'Not much,' said Mummy.

'How much?' asked Jeremy James.

'Not as much as it's hurting now,' said Mummy. 'And afterwards it'll stop hurting altogether.'

That didn't sound like a lot of hurt, but even a little hurt can be quite painful.

'How do you know how much it's hurting now?' he asked.

'Hmmmph!' said Mummy. 'Well, you said it was blooming agony, so it must be hurting quite a lot. Anyway, you stop worrying about it, and if you're a good boy and you don't cry, I'll give you a nice little bar of chocolate afterwards.'

Jeremy James would have preferred a nice big bar of chocolate, but even a little bar was worth not crying for.

Mr Pulham the dentist was a jolly looking man with a round face, and round spectacles, and a round body which was wrapped up in a long white coat. When the lady assistant took Jeremy James into the surgery (Mummy and the twins stayed in the waiting room), Mr Pulham was already smiling.

'Hello, Jeremy James,' said Mr Pulham, 'and how are you today?'

'I've got toothache,' said Jeremy James.

'Jolly good,' said Mr Pulham, and gave an even bigger smile.

'He's a little bit deaf,' whispered the assistant, 'so you'll have to speak louder.'

'*I've got toothache!*' shouted Jeremy James.

'Ah,' said Mr Pulham, 'then you've come to the right place. You come and sit here, then, Jeremy James.'

Jeremy James sat down in a big black shiny chair, and the lady assistant stood beside him and gave his hand a little squeeze.

'Hold tight,' said Mr Pulham, and pressed a button. Then Jeremy James suddenly found himself lying down instead of sitting up. Mr Pulham pressed another button, and Jeremy James felt the chair going up in the air.

'*Gosh, it's like a space rocket!*' shouted Jeremy James.

'That's right,' said Mr Pulham with a smile. 'For exploring the molar system. Now then, open wide.'

Jeremy James opened his mouth so wide that his face almost disappeared.

'My word,' said Mr Pulham, 'I could almost climb in there and walk around.'

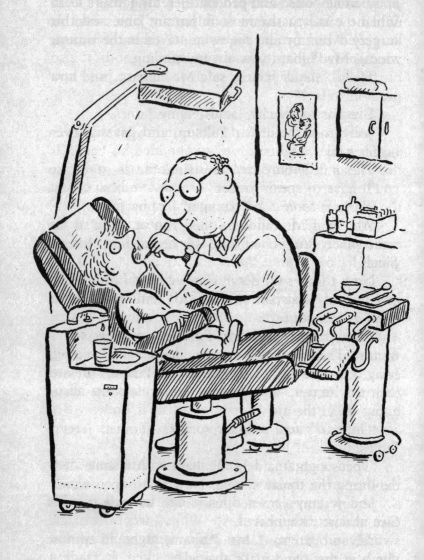

Then he poked and prodded Jeremy James's teeth until he came to the most important one, and this he poked and prodded even more than the others, which proved that it was a very special tooth. It also proved that the dentist knew just where to poke and prod.

'Glug!' said Jeremy James.

'Aha!' said the dentist. 'Oho, mhm, ts, ts.'

Then he straightened up and nodded his head. 'Is that the one, Jeremy James?' he asked.

'Yes,' said Jeremy James. 'I think I've been eating too many potatoes and too much cabbage.'

But the dentist didn't seem to hear, because he turned away and pulled over a long sharp instrument which let out a loud hum.

'Now then,' said Mr Pulham, 'what I'm holding here is a magic sword, called a drill. And inside your tooth is a nasty little dragon whose name is Decay. And that dragon is busy eating your tooth, and that's what's hurting you. So while the dragon's busy eating away, I'm going to creep up on him, and kill him with this magic sword. Only you must keep absolutely still, because if you move, he'll know we're after him and he'll hide away. Right?'

'Right,' said Jeremy James.

'Open up again,' said the dentist. 'And let's catch the dragon in the cave.'

And Jeremy James opened up the cave till his chin nearly tickled his chest. 'Whirr!' went the magic sword, and Jeremy James knew straight away that this was not the sort of magic he liked. It made a nasty noise, had a nasty feel, and gave off a nasty smell. The lady assistant squeezed his hand again.

'Whizz!' went the sword, and Jeremy James tried to think about the bar of chocolate he'd be getting when the dragon was dead.

And then suddenly the sword stopped humming.

'That's it,' said the dentist. 'Killed him dead as a denture. Wash him out now, Jeremy James.'

The assistant gave Jeremy James a glass. He washed out his mouth and saw little bits and pieces of something disappear down the pan.

'That didn't look much like a dragon,' said Jeremy James.

'What's that?' asked the dentist.

'*I said he didn't look much like a dragon!*' shouted Jeremy James.

'Nor would you if you'd had a fight with my magic sword,' said Mr Pulham. 'Now you lie back again, because we're going to have to fill in the hole the dragon made.'

So Jeremy James lay back while the dentist put some funny-tasting things in his mouth, and did a little more poking and prodding and scraping. Jeremy James thought about his bar of chocolate again, and decided that this was the easiest way of getting chocolate that he'd ever come across. All he had to do was lie still with his mouth open. And he reckoned he could lie still with his mouth open all day long if necessary. If Mummy were to offer him a really giant bar of chocolate, he could even

156

break the world record for lying still with his mouth open.

'Good lad,' said the dentist, taking all the funny things out of Jeremy James's mouth. 'Rinse it out again.'

The dentist went with Jeremy James to the waiting room, where Mummy sat holding Christopher in one arm and Jennifer in the other. She was joggling them up and down, and Jennifer was giggling, and Christopher was scowling.

'All done,' said Mr Pulham. 'Best patient I've had all day. He's as bright as a gold filling, aren't you, Jeremy James?'

'Well, it was quite easy,' said Jeremy James. 'I just thought about my bar of chocolate.

'What's that?' said the dentist. 'Now then, nothing to eat for two hours, and stay off the sweeties, Jeremy James, eh? Dragons always like sweet things, and you don't want any more dragons in there, do you?'

'Well, no-o, but . . .' Jeremy James didn't finish his sentence, because he wasn't quite sure what he wanted to say, and even if he had been, the dentist probably wouldn't have heard anyway.

'Mummy,' said Jeremy James, as he and Mummy pushed the twins homewards in the pram, 'will I have a bar of chocolate every time I go to the dentist's?'

'I shouldn't think so,' said Mummy. 'You heard what the dentist said – chocolate's bad for your teeth.'

'But if I *do* get another dragon in there, will you give me a bar of chocolate for not crying?'

'Maybe,' said Mummy – which was another typical Mummy reply. 'Let's hope you won't get any more dragons, though. You don't want any more of that blooming agony, do you?'

Jeremy James had to admit he would prefer to do without the blooming agony. But on the other hand, lying still with your mouth open was such a nice way of earning chocolate, and if you had to have a dragon before you could not-cry at the dentist's well . . . hmmph . . .

'Maybe,' said Jeremy James. 'We'll see.'

CHAPTER SIX

The Strike

Mummy, Jeremy James and the twins were out for a walk. The twins sat cushioned in their pram like a prince and princess in their carriage, Jeremy James pretended he was a racing driver and pushed them as fast as he could, and Mummy occasionally steered or braked when silly pedestrians got in the way. Of course Mummy didn't know that Jeremy James was the world champion driver who could *deliberately* miss toddlers, old men and fat ladies by a couple of inches when he wanted to – otherwise she would never have interfered.

They had almost reached the park when they heard the distant oompah-oompah of a brass band, and as Jeremy James wanted to see the soldiers, they walked on in the direction of the sound. However, there were no soldiers at all, but a band and a large crowd of ordinary men and women carrying banners and shouting things like: 'We want more!' and 'We want it now!' and 'Up with our wages!' and 'Down with the Government!' Mummy explained to Jeremy James that these were workers, and they were on

159

strike. Jeremy James wanted to know what 'on strike' meant, and Mummy explained that it meant not working. Then Jeremy James wanted to know how you could be a worker and not work, and Mummy said that was a very good question.

One of the workers who wasn't working got up on a box and shouted out 'Brothers!' till everyone was quiet. Jeremy James frowned in disbelief.

'They can't all be his brothers!' he said to Mummy. 'They'd never be able to get into the house.'

'They're not his real brothers,' said Mummy. 'It's just a way of talking.'

Jeremy James thought it was a silly way of talking, but as these were workers who didn't work, it was hardly surprising that they were also brothers who weren't brothers. Jeremy James wondered if the women were sisters who weren't sisters.

'Brothers,' said the man on the box, 'we need more money, we deserve more money, and we shall get more money!'

Everybody cheered, and Jeremy James cheered too, because he felt exactly the same way about his money. The man on the box went on to say that he was getting the same money as somebody else, but he should be getting more. Then a moment later he said somebody else was getting more money than he was, and that wasn't fair. And after that he said he didn't want more money than other people but he and other people should all have more money than everybody else, and nobody should have less than other people but everybody should get more and

160

then it would be fair. Jeremy James found it all rather hard to follow, but he cheered all the same because he was sure the man on the box was on his side.

On the way home, Jeremy James asked Mummy quite a lot of questions. For instance, he wanted to know just how the non-working workers would get the more money which they deserved. Mummy said that by not working, they hoped to force the people with the money to give them more. Jeremy James thought this meant that the less you worked, the more money you would get, but Mummy said it was all very complicated, and so Jeremy James reckoned it was just another way of talking, like the unworkers and the unbrothers.

'Why doesn't Daddy go on strike?' asked Jeremy James. 'Then he could get more money, too.'

'If Daddy went on strike,' said Mummy, 'nobody would notice any difference.'

That was also pretty hard for Jeremy James to understand. It seemed to him that there would be a big difference between Daddy locked away in his study, and Daddy sitting on the carpet playing trains and soldiers and cowboys. But grown-ups have their own ways of talking and thinking, and Jeremy James could only shake his head and wonder if, when he grew up, he would understand how grown-ups talked and thought.

At tea, Jeremy James sprang a little surprise on Mummy and Daddy. Mummy asked him to go and fetch a pot of jam.

'No,' said Jeremy James.

'Pardon?' said Mummy.

'I'm on strike,' said Jeremy James.

Mummy and Daddy looked at each other.

'This is very sudden,' said Daddy. 'You might have given us a warning.'

'I only just decided,' said Jeremy James. 'I think I deserve more money.'

'Aha,' said Daddy, 'don't we all!'

'And I'm not going to do any more work,' said Jeremy James, 'until my wages go up.'

'You'd better get that jam yourself, dear,' said Daddy to Mummy, 'we've got an industrial crisis on our hands. Now then, Jeremy James, what sort of wages were you thinking of?'

'A hundred pounds a week,' said Jeremy James. 'A hundred pounds and ... fourpence.'

'*And* fourpence,' said Daddy. 'Phew, that's pretty steep, with that fourpence.'

'Well I think I deserve it,' said Jeremy James. 'And other people shouldn't get more ... less ... more than me.'

'You mean,' said Mummy, 'you're not going to do any more work at all?'

'No,' said Jeremy James, 'except I might go outside and wave a flag and talk.'

'Who to?' asked Daddy.

'Some of the brothers,' said Jeremy James. 'You know, the brothers who aren't brothers.'

'Ah!' said Daddy. '*Those* brothers.'

When tea was finished, Mummy and Daddy

cleared the table, and Jeremy James went and sat in the armchair. Mummy and Daddy knew it was no use asking him to help, because people on strike don't help anyone – they just unwork until they get their money. He could hear them talking and laughing in the kitchen as they washed the dishes, and he smiled to himself because with a hundred pounds and fourpence he could buy tons and tons of chocolate and toys and sweets as well as a tricycle with a bell *and* a saddlebag, and all he had to do for the money was nothing – just hours and hours of nothing. Life couldn't be simpler.

At bedtime, Jeremy James kissed Mummy and Daddy goodnight, and – as they hadn't made any further mention of his strike or his money – he asked them when he would be getting his hundred pounds and fourpence.

'Can't tell you yet,' said Daddy. 'There'll have to be negotiations and committees of inquiry first, and we may even have to go to arbitration . . .'

Daddy always liked to make up long words when he didn't want to answer questions. Mummy just said 'Hmmph' and 'We'll see' and 'Goodnight, dear.'

As he lay in bed, Jeremy James wondered whether perhaps he shouldn't have asked for a bit more money. A hundred pounds and fourpence had seemed a lot at the time, but there must be people who got even more than that, and the man on the box had certainly said it wasn't fair if *anybody* got more than . . . or was it less than . . . anybody else. However, Jeremy James decided that if a hundred pounds

and fourpence wasn't enough, he could always go on strike again later.

The next morning, Mummy sprang a little surprise on Jeremy James. There was no breakfast.

'No breakfast?' said Jeremy James.

'I'm on strike,' said Mummy. 'Sorry, you'll have to go without.'

Sitting at the table was Daddy, and sitting in front of Daddy was a slippery fried egg and a crisp slice of bacon.

'No use looking at mine,' said Daddy. 'You'll have to get your own.'

'But I can't cook egg and bacon,' said Jeremy James.

'Awful, isn't it?' said Daddy. 'Let's hope Mummy's strike won't last too long.'

'Couldn't you cook it for me?' asked Jeremy James.

'Sorry,' said Daddy, 'I'm on strike, too.'

Jeremy James frowned. After all, if *everybody* went on strike, who was going to do the work?

'Well, what should I have for my breakfast?' he asked.

'Don't ask me,' said Mummy.

'That's up to you,' said Daddy. 'You can help yourself to a glass of water, can't you?'

For breakfast, Jeremy James had a glass of water, and a very dry crust of bread which he found at the bottom of an otherwise empty bread bin. It wasn't a very nice breakfast.

After the not-very-nice breakfast, Jeremy James waited to be told to go and do his Number Two. He had been looking forward to saying, 'No, I'm on strike', but Mummy and Daddy did not seem in the least bit interested. Mummy was reading a magazine and Daddy was reading the paper, and hours and hours went by.

'Aren't you going to tell me to do my Number Two?' asked Jeremy James.

'Of course not,' said Mummy. 'We're on strike.'

That was certainly not the conversation Jeremy James had looked forward to. Slowly, and rather miserably, he made his way upstairs. When he had not done his Number Two, and had not washed his face and not brushed his teeth, he looked round for his clothes. His dirty clothes were still where he had left them last night, but there were no clean clothes anywhere.

'Mummy,' called Jeremy James, 'I can't find any clean clothes.'

'I don't suppose there are any,' called Mummy. 'You'll have to wear your dirty ones.'

'But they're all muddy and horrible,' called Jeremy James.

'You'd better wash them out, then,' called Mummy. 'I'm on strike.'

Jeremy James went downstairs again.

'Still in your pyjamas?' said Daddy.

'You do look miserable,' said Mummy. 'What's the matter?'

'I didn't know *you* were going on strike,' said Jeremy James. 'I thought it was just going to be me.'

'Well, you gave us an idea,' said Mummy. 'And it does make life easier when you don't have to work, doesn't it?'

'When is your strike going to finish?' asked Jeremy James.

'When I get what I want,' said Mummy.

'What's that?' asked Jeremy James.

'I thought I'd ask for the same as you,' said Mummy. 'One hundred pounds and fourpence. We should both get the same, otherwise it wouldn't be fair.'

Jeremy James saw a glimmer of hope. 'Is Daddy going to give it to you?' he asked.

'No, *you* have to give it to me,' said Mummy.

'I'm only not working for you. I'm still working for Daddy and the twins.'

'But . . .' said Jeremy James, 'I haven't got a hundred pounds and fourpence.'

'Ah,' said Daddy, 'now I've had an idea about that. Supposing, Jeremy James, you were to end your strike, but instead of paying you your one hundred pounds and fourpence I gave it to Mummy instead, then it would be just like you paying Mummy, and so she could end her strike as well. How does that . . . um . . . strike you?'

Jeremy James thought about it, and the more he thought about it, the better it seemed.

'Will I be able to have my breakfast, then?' he asked.

'Of course,' said Daddy. 'That's part of the agreement.'

'And clean clothes?' asked Jeremy James.

'So long as you agree to the terms,' said Daddy. Jeremy James gave a smile as wide as a rasher of bacon, and his eyes shone as brightly as a newly fried egg.

'Yes, please,' he said.

'There you are,' said Daddy, 'all that's needed is goodwill and good sense on both sides, and industrial relations are simple as ABC.'

Jeremy James wasn't quite sure what 'industrial relations' were, but he did know that breakfast that day tasted nicer than it had ever tasted before.

closed. 'Hmmph!' he said, but still there was no attention.

'If I was Christopher or Jennifer,' thought Jeremy James, 'I could open my mouth and howl, and then Mummy would jump up and hug me and ask me what's the matter. But if I open my Jeremy James mouth and howl, all I shall get is a telling-off.'

Jeremy James gave a loud sigh, but still Mummy's eyes stayed shut.

Jeremy James would certainly have rolled over and died of boredom if, at that moment, there hadn't been a sudden dramatic event. The room was entered by a loud buzz. And in the middle of the buzz, carrying it all over the living room, was a nasty, bad-tempered, thoroughly dangerous wasp. It zoomed over Jeremy James's head, battered at the window like a shower of hailstones, and then came humming back across the room, right past Mummy and on to the arm of the settee. Surely Mummy would wake up now, with all that noise. But no, Mummy had heard nothing, and she couldn't know that just a few inches away from her leg crawled a yellow and black striped monster that might attack her at any minute. Perhaps he should wake her up to warn her. But would she be pleased or not? Jeremy James could imagine her saying: 'Oh thank you, Jeremy James, you've saved my life, what a good boy you are, here's a whole bar of chocolate!' But he could also imagine her saying 'Ts!' or 'Hmmph!' and 'Fancy waking me up for that!' It was a difficult decision to take, but he didn't have to take it because abruptly the wasp took off again and made a wasp-line for the window. And there it stayed, crawling up and down the glass, no doubt pleased to be out of the pouring rain.

Jeremy James tiptoed across the room and stood near, but not too near the window. The wasp didn't look quite so dangerous when it wasn't flying. In fact, it looked rather silly. It was waggling its black feelers up and down, and its little wings were as thin as tracing paper, and the yellow and black bit hardly seemed to belong to the wasp at all – it was just being dragged along behind, like Jeremy James when he went shopping with Mummy. Jeremy James decided that without its buzz, the wasp was a bit of a disappointment. He took one step nearer the window, stretched out his arm, stretched out one finger, and BUZZ! went the wasp, and whined straight past Jeremy James's left ear, so close that he even felt the draught. Jeremy James jumped back, and his heart was going thumpety-thump. Wasps *were* dangerous. And this wasp was particularly dangerous, because it was the sort of wasp that made you think it was silly but then suddenly leapt out at you when you weren't expecting it. Jeremy James reckoned a wasp like that could do a lot of damage if it was allowed to go on tricking people, and the person who managed to rid the world of such a dangerous animal would be a real hero, worthy of a hundred bars of chocolate.

The wasp continued to whizz from one side of the room to the other. It would take a lot of catching, a wasp that could whizz like that, but on the other

hand, wouldn't Mummy and Daddy be pleased when he showed them its dead body! Especially when they knew what a *dangerous* wasp it had been. Now what could he use to kill it? Mummy usually trod on insects she wanted to kill, but you couldn't tread on an insect that was whizzing round the room. The wasp hurtled past Jeremy James's right ear, and Jeremy James almost fell over as he got out of the way. This wasp was really looking for trouble, and it was going to be a question of who caught whom first. Jeremy James had an idea. He couldn't lift his leg up that high, but he could certainly lift his arm, and if he put his slipper on the end of his arm, well, the wasp wouldn't know the difference.

Jeremy James stood in the middle of the room,

slipper in hand, and waited. Zoom came the wasp, swish went the slipper, but the wasp was already a mile away. It was not going to be easy. Jeremy James tried a few random swishes, in the hope that the wasp might accidentally bump into the slipper, but his arm soon got tired and the wasp didn't have any accidents, so Jeremy James stopped swishing. Then Jeremy James lost sight and sound of the wasp. The room was completely silent, save for the gentle rise and fall of Mummy sleeping. Where was the enemy? Jeremy James stood quite still, eyes jerking as he scanned the ceiling, walls, floor and furniture. Had it gone? Was it hiding? Was it fast asleep somewhere? *Did* wasps go to sleep?

Jeremy James didn't like the silence. The wasp's buzz was nasty, but its silence was nastier. For all he knew, the wasp might be sitting just a couple of inches away, watching him and planning to sting him just when he wasn't looking. At least when it was whizzing around, you knew where it was, but if you didn't know where it was, it could be *anywhere*. It could even be on Jeremy James himself! Jeremy James had a quick look down at his body and legs. Then he twisted round to look at the back of his legs. No wasp. He humped his shoulders up and down. No buzz. All the same, he didn't feel safe. Very slowly and carefully, he padded round the room, slipper held high and eyes darting from side to side.

The wasp was not on the window. The wasp was not on the settee. The wasp was not on Mummy.

The wasp was not on either armchair. The wasp was not on the sideboard. The wasp was not . . . but it *was* . . . it was there, on the mantelpiece. To be precise, it was on the vase of flowers on the mantelpiece, waggling its feelers and ducking its silly black head. And it hadn't seen Jeremy James. It had no idea that it had been spotted, and it had no idea that Jeremy James was now creeping up behind it, slipper raised and heart pounding. Jeremy James padded closer and closer, an inch at a time, until he could actually see the wasp's black eyes and yellow cheeks, and its striped shopping bag quivering a little behind it. This was the most dangerous wasp that ever lived, and the safety of the world depended now on Jeremy James and his slipper. The great hunter paused, gathered all his strength together, and then in one swift movement brought his mighty weapon down on the back of his deadly enemy . . .

What happened next came as a terrible shock to Jeremy James, to Mummy, and above all to the wasp. There was a shattering crash as the vase came tumbling down from the mantelpiece and smashed to bits on the hearth below. In no time there were flowers and pools of water all over the living-room carpet, and Mummy had leapt off the settee with a face as white as a snowdrop.

'What was that?' she cried. 'What on earth was that?'

And then she saw what on earth it was, and she saw Jeremy James standing over the bits of vase and the mess of flowers and the puddles of water, and he

was holding a slipper in his hand, and he was looking up at her with eyes that were very round and rather frightened.

Before she could say a word, Daddy came bounding in.

'What on earth was that?' he said. 'I thought I heard a . . . Good Lord!'

And Daddy also saw the jumble of china and petals and leaves and soggy carpet.

'It's our best vase!' said Mummy.

'Well, it was,' said Daddy.

Mummy hurried out and came back carrying a cloth and a brush and a pan.

'What happened?' asked Daddy.

'There was a wasp,' said Jeremy James. 'It was a great big dangerous one.'

'And this great big dangerous wasp took a dislike to Mummy's vase,' said Daddy, 'and pushed it off the mantelpiece.'

'No,' said Jeremy James. 'I was trying to kill it.'

'I see,' said Daddy. 'But instead of killing the wasp, you killed the vase.'

'Well,' said Jeremy James, 'the wasp was sitting on the vase.'

'Aha,' said Daddy, 'so you hit the wasp and the vase.'

'Well, I'm not sure if I hit the wasp,' said Jeremy James.

'But we can be fairly sure that you hit the vase,' said Daddy.

'Yes,' said Jeremy James.

Mummy held up a tiny limp yellow and black thing. 'Is this your great big dangerous wasp?' she asked.

Jeremy James got down on his hands and knees and looked very closely. 'Yes,' he said, 'it is! That's the one! 'Cos it had those stripes!'

Daddy nodded thoughtfully. 'Not a bad shot, then,' he said.

'All the same,' said Mummy, 'in future, Jeremy James, leave the wasps alone.' Then she looked at Daddy. 'Vase today, window tomorrow.'

Daddy grinned. 'Lucky for you it didn't land on your nose,' he said.

'Oh I wouldn't have killed it if it had been on Mummy's nose,' said Jeremy James. 'Because that would have woken Mummy up.'

CHAPTER EIGHT

Pancakes and Blackberries

It was one of those warm, gentle September Saturdays which Daddy said were perfect for watching football and Mummy said were perfect for a family outing. Daddy wondered whether perhaps the family would like to go on an outing to a football match, but Mummy said she wouldn't, and Jeremy James said he'd prefer a place that sold strawberries and cream, and the twins said gurgle and glug, which meant they would go where they were taken. And so they were taken blackberry picking.

Daddy drove the whole family out into the country in their newly patched new car, and as they went down the narrow lanes, Mummy looked at the hedges on one side and Jeremy James looked at the hedges on the other, and Daddy tried to look at the hedges on both sides and the road in the middle. Sometimes when Daddy was looking at a hedge on one side, Mummy would take a look at the road in the middle and would shout out 'Watch it!' and Daddy would suddenly swing the steering wheel and say 'OK. Don't panic!' and Jeremy James would say 'There's some blackberries!' and Daddy would say 'Where?' and Mummy would say 'Keep your eye on the road!' and Daddy would swing the steering wheel again. Blackberry picking was quite exciting really.

At last, Daddy pulled up on a broad grass verge at the side of the road, and they all got out. Mummy put the twins in the pram, and Daddy fetched the baskets and sticks from the back of the car (the sticks were for pulling down brambles that were out of reach). All along the side of the road, the hedges were full of ripe berries, but what had attracted Jeremy James's attention was a tree-lined path just behind where Daddy had stopped the car. It was a very interesting path, because you couldn't see where it led to.

'Can I go and pick blackberries down there?' asked Jeremy James, and Mummy nodded, so off he went.

'Don't go too far away!' called Mummy.

Jeremy James wondered how far away too far away would be, but he just called out: 'I won't!' and carried on running.

There were no blackberries at all along the tree-lined path, but as there was a bend in the path, Jeremy James trotted on because – as Mummy kept saying to Daddy when Daddy took his eyes off the road – you never know what's round the bend. Round the bend, in fact, there were more trees and more bends, but still no blackberries. The only exciting thing along this path was the huge collection of what Daddy had once called 'pancakes'. 'Pancakes' were cows' Number Two, and a lot of cows had been along this path. Jeremy James quite enjoyed leaping over or swerving round the pancakes, because they were all very dangerous – even the old dried ones. If your foot just touched a tiny piece, there was certain to be a terrible explosion, and the whole world would go up in flames. You had to be very strong and very brave and very clever to avoid dangerous pancakes like these.

At last the tree-lined, pancake-carpeted path came to an end, and Jeremy James found himself in front of a high wooden gate which led into a huge green field. And on both sides of the gate, and all round the huge green field, there were thousands and thousands of blackberry bushes covered in millions and millions of blackberries. The blackberries outside the field were big and juicy, but the blackberries inside the field were even bigger and even juicier, and those – Jeremy James knew straight away – were without doubt the best blackberries in the world. Jeremy James reached through the bars of the gate and picked a berry. He popped it into his mouth. It was the sweetest, yummiest berry he had ever tasted. A second berry merely confirmed the impression made by the first, and a third berry merely confirmed the impression made by the second. Jeremy James could already taste the fruits of his labour as he squeezed through the wooden bars and into the green field.

What he had not noticed from outside – because they had been hidden from view by the thick

brambles – was a herd of cows in the green field. Most of them were on the far side, but there were a few fairly close, peacefully chewing the grass and swishing their tails from side to side. Jeremy James did not have a very high opinion of cows. They always moved so slowly, and they just chewed and stared and did their Number Two all over the place, and they said nothing but moo . . . cows were boring animals. You never saw cows at the zoo, because they just weren't interesting enough. You saw elephants at the zoo, because they were huge and tough and could whiffle things up with their noses. And you saw lions and tigers, because they could run fast and could roar. And you saw snakes and wolves and crocodiles, because they were deadly and frightening and interesting. You never saw boring old cows. Jeremy James shouted 'Moo!' at the cow that was nearest to him, but it just stood and blinked and went on chewing. The only dangerous thing about cows was their pancakes, but even they weren't interesting – just soft and smelly, like the twins' nappies. 'Moo!' said Jeremy James again, and stepped carefully towards the brambles.

The blackberries hung in glossy clusters from the bushes, and Jeremy James found it very hard to keep his eating up with his picking. But the most difficult part was avoiding the thorns. If you got pricked with one of those, you would go to sleep for a hundred years, and so you had to be very strong and very brave and very clever to keep your fingers away from them. Only a world champion picker could do it.

There were at least a dozen blackberries in Jeremy James's basket, and at least three dozen in his tummy, when he decided to have a rest. Blackberry picking is quite hard on the arms, let alone on the jaws, and so he turned round to talk with the cows. Some of them had come closer now, and there was one that was standing right in the middle of the field and was actually looking in Jeremy James's direction.

'Moo moo!' cried Jeremy James, but the cow neither mooed nor moved; it just stood there and stared.

'Cows are boring!' cried Jeremy James. 'Moo moo!'

The cow stood as still as a bottle of milk.

'You're too stupid even to be in a zoo!' cried Jeremy James. 'Moo moo! Zoo zoo!'

The cow suddenly lowered its head slightly and made a funny movement with its foot, as if wiping it on the grass.

'It stepped into a pancake!' giggled Jeremy James. 'Moo moo! Poo poo!'

The cow stopped wiping its foot, and took a few steps towards Jeremy James. Jeremy James stopped shouting poo poo and watched the cow. The cow watched Jeremy James.

'She knows what I'm saying,' thought Jeremy James. 'I can really speak cow language!' He took a deep breath, puffed out his chest till it was as round as a pancake, and let out the loudest moo ever to pass the lips of an uncow moo-speaker.

This seemed to have an extraordinary effect on the cow in the middle of the field, for it suddenly lowered its head almost to the ground, and began running at full speed straight towards Jeremy James. For a quarter of a second, Jeremy James stood watching the running cow, and in that quarter of a second a voice in his head told him that even if cows couldn't run, this one jolly well could, and if he didn't want to end up as a blackberry pancake, he had better start running too. Jeremy James dropped his basket and his stick, and dashed towards the gate. Behind him, he could hear loud thumps and a noise like a speeded-up Daddy's snore. He dived head first under the lowest wooden bar and scrambled out on to the path. Then without even stopping to look behind him, he raced away with legs whirling like propellers, and they carried him at world record

speed over the pancakes, past the trees, round the bends, on to the grass verge, and into Daddy's arms.

'Ouf!' said Daddy. 'And where are you running to?'

'It's a cow!' said Jeremy James, with a puff and a pant. 'A great big cow!'

'Cows won't hurt you,' said Daddy.

'This one will,' said Jeremy James. 'I said something it didn't like, and it ran after me. If I hadn't dived under the gate, it would have gobbled me up!'

'What did you say to it?' asked Daddy.

'Moo,' said Jeremy James.

'That sounds a reasonable thing to say to a cow,' said Daddy. 'Where's your basket?'

'I left it there,' said Jeremy James. 'And my stick. I dropped them when the cow ran after me.

'Jeremy James,' said Mummy, 'cows don't run after people.'

'This one did,' said Jeremy James.

'Come on, let's go and get your basket,' said Daddy.

Daddy took Jeremy James's hand, and they walked back up the path together.

'Now where is it?' asked Daddy.

'In the field,' said Jeremy James.

Daddy looked over the brambles at the cows quietly chewing the grass. 'Wait here, then,' he said, and climbed up the gate. He had just put his leg over the top when a great big cow raised its head and looked at him. Daddy looked back at the cow. Then Daddy looked a little more closely at the cow. And then Daddy brought his leg back, and climbed down the gate again.

'Aren't you going to get it?' asked Jeremy James.

'No,' said Daddy. Then he picked Jeremy James up in his arms and lifted him high. 'You see that nice cow over there,' he said. 'Well, it's got an udder underneath – like a glove turning into a balloon. But that not-so-nice cow over there hasn't got an udder. And do you know why? It's because he's not a cow at all – he's a bull. And if you ever see a bull in a field, Jeremy James, keep out. Right?'

Daddy humped Jeremy James over his shoulder and set off back down the path. Jeremy James raised his head to have a last look at the cow without an udder.

'Moo moo zoo zoo,' he murmured.

'What did you say to him?' asked Daddy.

'I told him he ought to be in a zoo,' said Jeremy James.

'And what did he say to that?' asked Daddy.

'I don't think he heard,' replied Jeremy James. 'I only said it quietly.'

CHAPTER NINE

The Ghost

It was a wild and stormy night. The thunder rumbled like the tummy of a hungry giant, the wind howled like fifty pairs of twins, and the rain rattled at the window like Daddy's typewriter in between pauses. From time to time Jeremy James's bedroom was lit by lightning, revealing Jeremy James himself sitting up in bed, wide-eyed, knees bent, shoulders hunched, with the blanket tightly wrapped around him.

Crash thump rumble rumble, went the thunder, and the curtains blew high into the room, whirling and flapping like ghosts chained to the wall. Jeremy James knew that they were curtains, and he knew that curtains are curtains and ghosts are ghosts, but he couldn't help wondering whether perhaps ghosts might *disguise* themselves as curtains, and whether perhaps these particular curtains might not be the ideal sort of curtains for ghosts to disguise themselves as.

Bang, bump, grumble, grumble, went the thunder, and Jeremy James wished he hadn't watched 'The Haunted House' on television that evening. Mummy had said he shouldn't because it would give him bad dreams, but Jeremy James had said he never had bad dreams, and Daddy had said he was a big boy now so maybe just this once . . . but Jeremy James didn't feel like a big boy now, and he was having very nasty dreams even though he wasn't asleep. All those creaking doors and dark shadows and floating figures and loud screams and whispering voices and wild stormy nights just like this one . . . What was that?

Jeremy James sat even more up than he had been sitting before.

Creak, said the floorboards outside his bedroom door.

Crack, boom, mumble mumble, went the thunder, and ratatat went the rain, and howl went the wind – but definitely creak went the floorboards. And then click went the door handle. And squeak-creak went the door. Jeremy James felt himself go all cold, and his body went as stiff as a block of ice, and he rolled his eyes sideways to try and see what was happening, because he couldn't even turn his head, which had somehow got locked on to his shoulders. In the darkness he could just make out the dim shape of the door as it slowly swung open. And into the room floated a figure in a long robe that glowed with an eerie light. There was a flash that illuminated the whole room for a second, and Jeremy James froze into an even stiffer block of ice as he saw the face of the ghost: it was a skull! He saw the white cheeks and the hollow shadows of the eyes, and on

top of the skull he saw a kind of crown – but then everything was dark again, and Jeremy James wished the floor would open up so that he could drop down into the living room and be safe. It was no use calling out for Mummy or Daddy, because the ghost would hear, and the ghost was nearer to him than Mummy or Daddy. It would get him long before they could come. Maybe the ghost hadn't seen him. He could still hide.

Slowly, very slowly Jeremy James eased himself down the bed, covering his tummy, then his chest, then his arms ... Where was it? Ah, there it was, right at the foot of the bed. Was it going past the bed? Yes, it was moving, slowly, silently, away towards the window. Jeremy James could see the curtain-ghosts reaching out towards the new ghost, and a little beam of warm hope shone into his frozen brain: perhaps the ghost didn't even know about Jeremy James; perhaps it only knew about the curtain-ghosts. It had only come to join the others.

The ghost went all the way to the window, and Jeremy James turned his head to watch, and he must have turned his body a little as well because kerdoing went the bed-springs and then swish went the curtain-ghosts, and split, roll, hmmph hmmph, went the thunder, and ... 'Are you awake, Jeremy James?' came a strange, cold, whispering voice.

'N ... n ... no,' said Jeremy James. 'I'm as ... s ... sleep.'

But the ghost didn't believe him. And as another flash of lightning lit up the crowned skull and the shiny robe, Jeremy James saw the ghost floating away from the window and towards his bed.

'Yarrk!' gulped Jeremy James, and pulled the covers right over his head. So long as he couldn't see the ghost, he reckoned, the ghost couldn't see him. But the ghost began to tug at the covers, and he could hear its whispery voice and feel its clammy fingers . . . but he held on tight, keeping the blankets over his face and his ears, and rolling his body into a little ball like a hedgehog without any spikes.

The ghost whispered and tugged for a little while longer, but then seemed to give up. Jeremy James could hear and feel nothing there at all. Then . . . Clatter! That wasn't the wind or the rain or the thunder. It sounded as if it came from the window. Jeremy James wanted to look, but didn't dare. He just held on tight and listened. Nothing. Wait! A squeaky creak . . . then a click. That must be the door. Had the ghost gone? Or was it a trick just to make him come out? You never know with ghosts – one moment they're gone and the next they're with you again. Jeremy James stayed quite still in his safe hiding place. He counted all the way up to twenty, and then up to ten again just to make sure. Then he slowly loosened his grip on the blankets – not completely, because he had to be ready to pull them tight if the ghost attacked again, but just enough to make the ghost think he was relaxing. Nothing happened. Still safe. Jeremy James very, very slowly lifted the blankets, and very, very slowly poked his whole head out from underneath. And still nothing happened.

Now, even less slowly, and in fact quite quickly, Jeremy James poked an arm out from under the covers and reached for the light switch at the side of the bed. He'd been told it was to be used in emergencies, like wanting to do a wee in the middle of the night. This was certainly more important than doing a wee in the night. On went the light. There was no ghost. And the door was closed. He looked round the room till his gaze rested on the window. The curtains – they were still! So the curtain-ghosts had gone, too! That must be it: the ghost had come to collect his friends, and they'd all gone out together. And if Jeremy James hadn't had the presence of mind to dive beneath the blankets and fight them off, they would have taken him with them.

Jeremy James sat up in bed and felt very pleased with himself. There can't be many boys, he thought, who have fought off a ghost and lived to tell the tale. Perhaps there would be a film about it tomorrow on the television. He would have liked to go and tell Mummy and Daddy about it straight away, but perhaps if he opened the bedroom door ... well, you never knew what you might find out on the landing. He'd tell them tomorrow.

Plunk, pop, mm mm, went the thunder, which suddenly seemed quite a long way away. And the wind seemed to be whimpering, and the rain to be lightly pattering. The night wasn't at all frightening really. You just need a little bit of courage, and even

192

ghosts will leave you alone. Jeremy James smiled to himself, pinned an imaginary medal to his chest, and suddenly felt rather sleepy. He put out the light, curled up into a little ball, and – just to make quite sure he was safe – pulled the covers up over his head.

'I saw a ghost last night,' said Jeremy James at breakfast.

'Did you, dear?' said Mummy, presenting him with down-to-earth bacon and eggs. 'That must have been nice.'

'No, it wasn't,' said Jeremy James. 'It was a bit frightening. Well, it would have been frightening if I'd been frightened.'

'But you weren't frightened, eh?' said Daddy over the top of the newspaper.

'No,' said Jeremy James.

'Good for you,' said Daddy.

'It had a long white robe on, and a crown, and its face was a skull,' said Jeremy James, 'and it knew my name, 'cos it spoke to me in a horrible whispery voice.'

'When was this, dear?' asked Mummy.

'Last night,' said Jeremy James. 'During the storm. It came into my room and tried to take me away.'

'What did you say it looked like?' asked Daddy.

'It had a crown on,' said Jeremy James, 'and its face was a skull, and it was wearing a shiny robe.'

Daddy's face suddenly broke into a big grin. And

when Jeremy James looked at Mummy, she was grinning, too.

'It wasn't funny,' said Jeremy James. 'I could have been killed!'

But then they started laughing, and they went on laughing until they just couldn't laugh any more.

'That ghost,' said Daddy, puffing and wiping his eyes, 'do you know who it was, Jeremy James?'

'It was a dead king,' said Jeremy James. 'That's who it was.'

'It was me,' said Mummy, 'in my nightdress. I had white cream over my face, and I was wearing curlers. I always put them in before I go to bed!'

'Mummy came in to close your window,' said Daddy. 'Because of the storm.'

And Jeremy James sat there while Mummy and Daddy laughed out their last howls of laughter. And then they stopped laughing, and Mummy gave Jeremy James a big hug.

'But weren't you brave!' she said. 'You were so brave that it never occurred to me you might be frightened.'

'I wasn't frightened,' said Jeremy James.

'That's what I mean,' said Mummy. 'You *are* a brave boy.'

'Well, I can tell you,' said Daddy, 'when I see Mummy in face cream and curlers, it frightens *me*.'

And as a special reward for his extraordinary bravery, Jeremy James was given a shiny 50p piece, and permission to spend it on a bar of chocolate.

Which only goes to show that even if parents do the strangest things most of the time, they do just occasionally have some connection with the real world.

CHAPTER TEN

Father Christmas and Father Christmas

Jeremy James first met Father Christmas one Saturday morning in a big shop. He was a little surprised to see him there, because it was soon going to be Christmas, and Jeremy James thought Santa Claus really ought to be somewhere in the North Pole filling sacks with presents and feeding his reindeer. However, there he was, on a platform in the toy department, handing out little parcels to the boys and girls who came to see him.

'Here you are, Jeremy James,' said Daddy, and handed him a £1 coin.

'What's that for?' asked Jeremy James.

'To give to Santa Claus,' said Daddy. 'You have to pay to go and see him. I'll wait for you here.'

Daddy stood rocking the twins in the pram, while Jeremy James joined the end of a long queue of children. (Mummy was busy studying turkeys in the food department.) Jeremy James thought it rather odd that he had to pay for Santa Claus. It was as if Santa Claus was a bar of chocolate or a packet of liquorice allsorts.

196

'Do we really have to pay £1 to see him?' he asked a tall boy in front of him.

'Yeah,' said the tall boy. 'An' he'll prob'ly give you a plastic car worth 10p.'

Jeremy James stood on tiptoe to try and catch a glimpse of Father Christmas. He could just see him, all wrapped up in his red cloak and hood, talking to a little girl with pigtails. It certainly was him – there was no mistaking the long white beard and the rosy cheeks. It was really quite an honour that Santa Claus should have come to this particular shop out of all the shops in the world, and perhaps he needed the £1 to help pay for his long journey. Jeremy James looked across towards Daddy, and they gave each other a cheery wave.

As Jeremy James drew closer to Santa Claus, he felt more and more excited. Santa Claus seemed such a nice man. He was talking to each of the children before he gave them their present, and he would pat them on the head and sometimes let out a jolly laugh, and only once did he seem at all un-Father-Christmas-like; that was when a tall scruffy boy stepped up before him and said he hadn't got £1 but he wanted a present all the same. Then Father Christmas pulled a very serious face and Jeremy James distinctly heard him ask the boy if he would like a thick ear, which seemed a strange sort of present to offer. The boy wandered off grumbling, and when he was some distance away stuck his tongue out at Santa Claus, but by then the next child was on the platform and

the jolly smile had returned as the hand reached out for the £1 coin.

Jeremy James noticed, with a slight twinge of disappointment, that the presents really were rather small, but as Santa Claus had had to bring so many, perhaps he simply hadn't had room for bigger ones. It was still quite exciting to look at the different shapes and the different wrappings and try to guess what was inside them, and by the time Jeremy James came face to face with the great man, his eyes were shining and his heart was thumping with anticipation.

'What's your name?' asked Santa Claus in a surprisingly young voice.

'Jeremy James,' said Jeremy James.

198

'And have you got £1 for Santa Claus?'

'Yes,' said Jeremy James, handing it over.

Then Santa Claus gave a big smile, and his blue eyes twinkled out from below his bushy white eyebrows, and Jeremy James could see his shining white teeth between the bushy white moustache and the bushy white beard. All the bushy whiteness looked remarkably like cotton wool, and the redness on the cheeks looked remarkably like red paint, which made Jeremy James feel that Santa Claus really was very different from everybody else he knew.

'Is it for your reindeer?' asked Jeremy James.

'What?' asked Santa Claus.

'The £1,' said Jeremy James.

'Ah,' said Santa Claus, 'ah well . . . in a kind of a sort of a manner of speaking as you might say. Now then Jeremy James, what do you want for Christmas?'

'Oh, I'd like a tricycle, with a bell *and* a saddle-bag. Is that what you're going to give me?'

'Ah no, not exactly,' said Santa Claus, 'not now anyway. Not for £1, matey. But here's a little something to keep you going.' And Santa Claus handed him a little oblong packet wrapped in Father-Christmassy paper.

'Thank you,' said Jeremy James. 'And do you really live in the North Pole?'

'Feels like it sometimes,' said Santa Claus. 'My landlord never heats the bedrooms. Off you go. Next!'

Jeremy James carried his little packet across to

where Mummy had joined Daddy to wait with the twins.

'Open it up then,' said Daddy.

Jeremy James opened it up. It was a little box. And inside the little box was a plastic car.

'Worth at least 5p,' said Daddy.

'Ten,' said Jeremy James.

Jeremy James's second meeting with Santa Claus came a week and a day later. It was at a children's party in the church hall. The party began with the Reverend Cole hobbling on to the platform and saying several times in his creaky voice that he hoped everyone would enjoy himself, and the party was to end with Santa Claus coming and giving out the presents. In between, there were games, eating and drinking, and more games. As soon as the first lot of games got underway, the Reverend Cole hobbled out of the hall, and nobody even noticed that he'd gone. The games were very noisy and full of running around, and as Jeremy James was extremely good at making a noise and running around, he enjoyed himself.

The eating and drinking bit came next, and Jeremy James showed that he was just as good at eating and drinking as he was at making a noise and running around. In fact, Mummy, who was one of the helpers (having left Daddy at home to mind the twins and the television set), actually stopped him when he was on the verge of breaking the world record for the number of mince pies eaten at a single go. When at last there was not a crumb left on any of the tables, the helpers cleared the empty paper plates and the empty paper cups and the not so empty wooden floor. After a few more games full of shrieks and squeaks and bumps and thumps, all the children had completely forgotten about Santa Claus, but Santa Claus had not forgotten them. At the stroke of six o'clock, one of the grown-ups called for everyone to keep quiet and stand still, and at ten past six, when everyone was quiet and standing still, the hall door opened, and in came Father Christmas.

The first thing Jeremy James noticed about Father Christmas was how slowly he walked – as if his body was very heavy and his legs were weak. He was wearing the same red coat and hood as before, and he had a white beard and moustache, but ... somehow they were not nearly so bushy. His cheeks were nice and red, but ... he was wearing a pair of spectacles. And when he called out to the children: 'Merry Christmas, everyone, and I hope you're enjoying yourselves!' his voice was surprisingly creaky and hollow-sounding.

Jeremy James frowned as Santa Claus heaved himself and his sack up on to the platform. There was definitely something strange about him. The other children didn't seem to notice, and they were all excited as the helpers made them line up, but perhaps the others had never met Santa Claus before, so how could they know?

Jeremy James patiently waited for his turn, and

when it came, he stepped confidently up on to the platform.

'Now . . . er . . . what's your name?' asked Santa Claus, peering down at Jeremy James.

'You should remember,' said Jeremy James. 'It was only a week ago that I told you.'

'Oh dear,' said Santa Claus. 'I do have a terrible memory.'

'And a week ago,' said Jeremy James, 'you weren't wearing glasses, and your voice wasn't all creaky like it is now.'

'Oh,' said Santa Claus, 'wasn't I . . . er . . . wasn't it?'

Jeremy James looked very carefully at Santa Claus's face, and Santa Claus looked back at Jeremy James with a rather puzzled expression in his . . . brown eyes.

'Santa Claus has blue eyes!' said Jeremy James.

'Oh!' said Santa Claus, his mouth dropping open in surprise.

'And he's got white teeth, too!' said Jeremy James.

'Hm!' said Santa Claus, closing his mouth in dismay.

'You're not Santa Claus at all,' said Jeremy James. 'You're not!'

And so saying, Jeremy James turned to the whole crowd of children and grown-ups, and announced at the top of his voice.

'He's a cheat! He's not Father Christmas!'

Father Christmas rose unsteadily to his feet, and

as he did so, his hood fell off, revealing a shiny bald head. Father Christmas hastily raised a hand to pull the hood back on, but his hand brushed against his beard and knocked it sideways, and as he tried to save his beard, he brushed against his moustache, and that fell off altogether, revealing beneath it the face of . . . the Reverend Cole.

'There!' said Jeremy James. 'That proves it!'

One or two of the children started crying, but then the man who had been organizing the games jumped up on to the platform and explained that the real Santa Claus was very busy preparing for Christmas, and that was why the Reverend Cole had had to take his place. They hadn't wanted to disappoint the children. And it was just bad luck that there'd been such a clever boy at the party, but the clever boy should be congratulated all the same on being so clever, and if they could just go on pretending that the Reverend Cole was the real Santa Claus, the clever boy should have two presents as a special reward for being so clever.

Then the Reverend Cole put on his beard and moustache and hood again, and everybody clapped very loudly as Jeremy James collected his two presents. And they were big presents, too – a book of bible stories, and a set of paints and brushes. As Jeremy James said to Mummy on the way home:

'It's funny that the real Santa Claus only gave me a rotten old car for £1, but Mr Cole gave me these big presents for nothing.'

But as Father Christmas was a grown-up, and

the Reverend Cole was also a grown-up, Jeremy James knew there was no point in trying to understand it all. Grown-ups never behave in the way you'd expect them to.

CHAPTER ELEVEN

Waiting for Christmas

'The trouble with Christmas,' said Jeremy James, 'is the time in between.'

'In between what?' said Mummy, tinselling the Christmas tree.

'Well, in between whenever it is and Christmas,' said Jeremy James. 'Like in between today and Christmas. If there wasn't time in between, it would be Christmas now, and I wouldn't have to wait for my presents.'

'Ouch!' said Daddy, sticking a pin into a paper chain and a thumb. 'Blooming pins . . . never go where you want them to go.'

It was ever such a long time before Christmas – in fact a whole week. The world outside was like a giant birthday cake, covered with icing-snow, candle-trees, and houses made of candy. People walking down the street were all muffled up, showing nothing but their red cheeks and their shining eyes and their steam-engine puffs of breath. Inside, it was cosy and warm, and Mummy had been busy bathing and feeding the twins, cleaning the house, cooking the lunch

and decorating the Christmas tree, while Daddy had been putting up a paper chain. Paper chains were difficult things to put up. Especially when Daddy was putting them up. They seemed to have minds of their own when Daddy put them up: while he stuck one end to the wall, the other end would curl round his arm and his neck, so that he could only straighten it out by unsticking the end he had stuck, but then when he'd unstuck that end, it would also twine round his other arm, and he would finish up by having to break the paper chain in the middle in order to find his arms again. Daddy didn't like paper chains, and paper chains didn't seem too fond of Daddy.

'Mummy,' said Jeremy James. 'Daddy's sucking his thumb again.'

'I can see we shall have to put another plaster on it,' said Mummy.

'Pin went practically right through it,' said Daddy. 'Another millimetre and you could have put me in somebody's butterfly collection.'

'Well,' said Mummy, 'let's hope you'll recover in time to get that paper chain up before Christmas.'

'How far away *is* Christmas?' asked Jeremy James.

'Just ten minutes less than when you last asked,' said Mummy. 'A week, dear. Seven days and seven nights.'

'Well I don't think I can wait that long,' said Jeremy James. 'They should make it come earlier.'

'You can have your presents tomorrow if you like,' said Daddy. 'Only won't you be disappointed next week, when everybody else is getting presents and you're getting nothing!'

'You could have yours, too!' said Jeremy James.

'No thank you,' said Daddy. 'Otherwise we'll finish up celebrating the New Year with Easter eggs.'

Jeremy James was bursting to give Mummy and Daddy their presents. He wanted to give them their presents almost as much as he wanted them to give him his. He had saved up for ages and ages, and had given a great deal of thought to these presents, and he had bought them today all by himself at the sweet shop round the corner. Now they were nestling in a very secret place where no one would ever dream of looking: under his bed. There were two presents – one, a bright box of liquorice allsorts with a robin on it, and the other, a thick bar of chocolate with Santa Claus on it. And the only problem Jeremy James had with these two perfect presents was to decide which one he should give to whom. He could easily imagine Mummy opening the bright box and saying, 'Here, Jeremy James, have a liquorice allsort.' But he could just as easily imagine her breaking the thick bar of chocolate and saying, 'Here, Jeremy James, have a piece of chocolate.' On the other hand, he could hear Daddy saying, 'Here, Jeremy James, have some liquorice allsorts.' But Daddy would also say, 'Here, Jeremy James, have some chocolate.' It was a very difficult decision indeed.

Mummy's Christmas tree was looking more and more like an enchanted forest, and Daddy's paper chain was looking more and more like confetti. It might be best to concentrate on Mummy. There were two things Jeremy James wanted to know: would Mummy prefer chocolate or liquorice allsorts, and what was Jeremy James getting for Christmas? They were very easy questions for Mummy to answer, but Jeremy James knew from experience that grown-ups didn't like answering questions. For instance, he'd asked Mummy how the twins had got into her stomach, but she hadn't told him, though she must have known because, after all, it was *her* stomach. And he'd asked Daddy how much money he'd got, but Daddy hadn't told him, though he must have known because, after all, it was *his* money. Grown-ups are very quick at asking you and ordering you and stopping you and starting you, but when it comes to answering you, they can be very slow indeed.

'Mummy,' said Jeremy James, casually poking a holly berry with his toe, 'which do you think is nicer, chocolate or liquorice allsorts?'

'They're both nice,' said Mummy.

'Yes, but which is *nicer*?' said Jeremy James.

'Well, sometimes chocolate, and sometimes liquorice allsorts,' said Mummy. 'It depends what you feel like.'

'Which do *you* usually feel like?' asked Jeremy James.

Mummy thought long and hard. 'Well,' she said, 'in the afternoons, liquorice allsorts, and in the evenings chocolate.'

Grown-ups can be very annoying at times. Jeremy James made one more effort: 'What about the mornings?'

'In the mornings,' said Mummy, 'I don't really feel like sweets at all.'

Jeremy James wandered over to Daddy.

'Daddy,' he said, 'which do you prefer – chocolate or liquorice allsorts?'

Daddy seemed quite pleased to see Jeremy James, and he stopped work at his paper chain in order to consider the question.

'Well,' he said, 'I prefer chocolate to those pink liquorice allsorts with black in the middle, but I prefer those black liquorice allsorts with white in the middle to chocolate. But by and large, all in all, and as a whole, I think I'd say it's fifty-fifty.'

Jeremy James's face became as long as Santa Claus's beard.

'Which do *you* prefer?' asked Daddy.

Jeremy James's face shortened again. 'That's easy,' he said. 'Both.'

Mummy had finished the Christmas tree, and it sparkled like diamonds and emeralds.

'I'll give you a hand with those paper chains now,' she said to Daddy.

'Thanks,' said Daddy. 'Blooming awkward things. You can't really do them on your own.'

'No, you can't,' said Mummy, with rather more emphasis on 'you' than on 'can't'.

Jeremy James put his hands in his pockets and wandered over to the living-room door. His first question had been well and truly non-answered, and there seemed little point in asking the second. 'Wait and see,' they'd say, or 'You'll know on Christmas Day.' But at the last moment, he decided to ask it all the same.

'What *am* I going to have for Christmas?' he said.

'Wait and see,' said Daddy.

'You'll know on Christmas Day,' said Mummy.

Grown-ups are very predictable.

Daddy went on showing Mummy how paper chains *should* be put up, and then Mummy started showing Daddy how paper chains *could* be put up. Jeremy James wandered out of the room and up the stairs. He peeped into the twins' room, but

211

Christopher and Jennifer were both fast asleep, and even if they hadn't been fast asleep, they wouldn't have been able to help him. Babies weren't much help to anybody. All they could do was eat, sleep, cry and bring up wind. And make their nappies dirty. Babies, as far as Jeremy James was concerned, were as useless as empty wrappers, and he couldn't see why grown-ups made such a fuss of them.

Jeremy James went into his own room, knelt down, and pulled two packets out from under the bed. There was no doubt about it, they were very attractive packets, and it made your mouth water just to look at them. It would make your mouth water even more to look at what was inside the packets. Mummy and Daddy were in for a real treat at Christmas. You couldn't have a nicer treat than chocolate and liquorice allsorts. Unless, of course, there was something *wrong* with the chocolate and the liquorice allsorts. For instance, the chocolate people might have accidentally wrapped up a block of wood by mistake, and the liquorice allsorts people might have filled the box with pebbles or marbles by mistake. These things do happen sometimes. Mummy had once found a piece of string in her soup, and Daddy was always finding little insects in his brussels sprouts, and if the soup people and the brussels sprout people can make mistakes like that, who knows what the chocolate people and the liquorice allsort people might get up to? It was definitely safer for Jeremy James to have a quick look at what was *inside* the packets.

Inside the chocolate wrapper there was chocolate. Thick, dark, smooth-looking chocolate, with ridges in between the squares where you could break bits off. Jeremy James wondered if the chocolate would taste as nice as it looked. You could never tell by the way things looked. After all, when he'd had a cough a few weeks ago, Mummy had brought out a bottle with a lovely-looking red liquid in it, but the lovely-looking red liquid had tasted all ug-yuk-yucky, and he'd have spat it out if Mummy hadn't made him swallow it. No, you could never be sure that nice-looking things tasted nice. The only way to be sure was to try them for yourself. And you could always fold the silver paper over afterwards, to hide the bit that was missing... And no one would notice if there were two or three liquorice allsorts missing from the box, because all the other liquorice allsorts would roll together and fill the gap . . . The chocolate and the liquorice allsorts did taste nice – in fact, they tasted delicious. All of them.

That night, which was just a week before Christmas, Jeremy James had a very bad tummy ache. Nobody else in the family had a tummy ache but, as Daddy said, it could just have been the excitement. Fortunately he was quite all right again after a couple of days, but every so often Mummy and Daddy noticed a slightly worried look on Jeremy James's face – especially when the talk came round to the subject of Christmas presents. But by Christmas Eve the worried frown had completely disappeared, and Jeremy James simply could not stop talking about Christmas presents. He couldn't wait to get his presents, and he couldn't wait to give his presents, and he wished time wouldn't pass so slowly, and he wouldn't sleep tonight, but he'd wait up for Santa Claus, and he wished he knew what Santa Claus was going to bring him, and would Mummy and Daddy like to know what Jeremy James had got them? He could tell them now if they liked. And he wouldn't mind if they told him what they were going to give him. He wouldn't mind giving *and* getting his presents straight away. No? Tomorrow? Oooooh, all right, then. But supposing tomorrow didn't come?

*

Tomorrow came, and it was the best Christmas there had ever been. Santa Claus had left a whole lot of apples and oranges and picture books and toys and sweets in Jeremy James's empty pillowcase, and he'd left more toys and nice clothes for the twins, and when Jeremy James went down to the living room – which was like fairyland with that sparkling tree and all those firmly fastened paper chains – he found an enormous parcel at the foot of the tree. Inside, there was the shiniest new tricycle with a bell *and* a saddle-bag. But the most unusual presents were the presents Jeremy James gave Mummy and Daddy. For Mummy there was a beautiful box with a pretty little robin on its lid. And inside the box were lots of pebbles, which Jeremy James had very carefully picked up at the bottom of the garden. And for Daddy there was a beautiful packet with a smiling Santa Claus on top and silver paper underneath, and inside the packet was a lovely block of wood (found in Daddy's tool shed) with a picture of Daddy on it, drawn by Jeremy James himself. And although Mummy did make a little sound rather like 'Hmmph' when she first saw the box and Daddy's packet, she and Daddy smiled at each other, gave Jeremy James a big thank-you kiss, and agreed that, without a doubt, their presents had been well worth waiting for.

CHAPTER TWELVE

The Christmas Spirit

'The trouble with Christmas,' said Jeremy James, 'is the time after.'

'The time after what?' asked Mummy, undressing the Christmas tree.

'After Christmas,' said Jeremy James.

'I thought it was the time between,' said Daddy, struggling to unravel himself from a paper chain which seemed reluctant to be taken down.

'No, the time in between's all right really,' said Jeremy James, 'because you can look forward to getting your presents then. Only with the time after, you can't look forward any more.'

'That's true,' said Daddy, 'unless you look forward to *next* Christmas.'

'That's too long,' said Jeremy James.

'Like this blooming paper chain,' said Daddy. 'More like a boa-constrictor than a paper chain.'

'I think we should have Christmas every day,' said Jeremy James, 'so that we can enjoy ourselves all the time.'

'If it was Christmas every day,' said Mummy, 'there'd never be any work done.'

It was a typical grown-up remark. They seemed to think work was all that mattered, and playing and enjoying yourself were not important. Life was all meat, potatoes and cabbage to them, with a tiny dollop of ice cream if there was time. They didn't seem to realize that they were much *happier* playing games and giving one another presents, and Jeremy James was much happier too, and all they had to do was pretend every day was Christmas and they could live happily ever after. What was the point of working if it stopped you from enjoying yourself?

'Why do you have to do work?' asked Jeremy James.

'Good question,' said Daddy. 'I sometimes ask myself the same thing.'

'Because if Daddy didn't work,' said Mummy, 'there'd be no money to pay for our house and our food and our clothes and everything else. And if I didn't work, you'd have nothing to eat and nothing to wear. You didn't like it when we went on strike, did you? And that's how it would be all the time.'

'Well, maybe you should just work every one day, and then have Christmas every next day,' said Jeremy James. 'That would be fair.'

Daddy agreed, and Mummy said perhaps they'd do that when their ship came home, and Jeremy James said he didn't know they had a ship, and Mummy said that was just another way of saying when they were very rich, and Daddy said it was another way of saying pigs would fly.

'Anyway,' said Daddy, 'I agree with Jeremy James. If we celebrated Christmas all the year round, people would be happier, the world would be brighter, and I wouldn't have to keep fighting these blooming paper chains.'

There was no doubt that Christmas was well and truly over. The turkey, Christmas pudding and mince pies were all finished, the decorations were coming down, the cards and parcels had stopped arriving, and even the crisp white snow had given way to dirty grey slush. It was as if the whole world had decided to be miserable. It made Jeremy James feel quite depressed, until he was suddenly struck by an interesting idea:

'Will the shops be open again now?' he asked.

'Yes,' said Mummy.

'Aha!' said Jeremy James. The interesting idea looked even more interesting. 'I've got some money upstairs,' said Jeremy James. 'Left over from Christmas.'

'Have you?' said Mummy.

'Yes,' said Jeremy James.

There was a moment's silence. Mummy didn't seem to have realized that Jeremy James had had an interesting idea.

'If the shops are open,' said Jeremy James, 'I could go and spend some of my money, couldn't I?'

'I haven't got time to go shopping now, dear,' said Mummy, who had finished taking decorations off the Christmas tree and was now taking decorations off Daddy.

'Well, can I just go to the sweetshop round the corner, then?' asked Jeremy James.

'Yes, I suppose so,' said Mummy. 'Only you'd better not spend more than 50p.'

That made the interesting idea a little less interesting than it had been, but still, you could buy a lot of nice sweets with 50p – 50p worth, in fact.

'Can I go on my new tricycle?' asked Jeremy James.

'As long as you don't go in the road,' said Mummy.

'It's pavement all the way,' said Daddy. 'But don't go knocking down old ladies or garden walls, and don't break the speed limit.'

The interesting idea became an interesting reality. Jeremy James, muffled up in scarf and overcoat, slipped a few shining coins into his shining leather saddlebag, tinkled loudly on his shining silver bell, and set out through the splashy, squelchy, slithery slush to break the world tricycle record between home and the sweetshop. There was nobody on the pavement at all, and with a loud brrm Jeremy James gathered speed, his legs whirling round like pink catherine wheels. As he neared the corner, he slowed down a little, swung the handlebars round, let out a loud 'Errgh' worthy of any world champion driver, and raced headlong into a great mass of brown stuff that was all soft and crumply and made a noise very similar to Jeremy James's 'Errgh' only louder and

deeper. When the soft crumply mass of brown stuff had picked itself up off the pavement, it turned out to be a man in a brown overcoat. The man in the brown overcoat wasn't too pleased at his first meeting with Jeremy James, and as he brushed the wet slush off himself, he looked rather fiercely at the tricycle and its rider, and said:

'You wanner look where you're goin' with that thing. I could 'ave been killed. Dead.'

'I'm ever so sorry,' said Jeremy James. 'I didn't see you.'

'Not many people *can* see round corners,' said the man in the brown overcoat. 'That's why you should go slow round corners. So you don't bump into people an' kill 'em dead.'

The man in the brown overcoat was fairly old, and his coat was very old, because it was all torn and thready. When he'd stopped looking fiercely at Jeremy James, his face became kinder, though it was covered in spiky bristles and didn't seem very clean.

'Got that for Christmas, did you?' he said, nodding towards the tricycle.

'Yes,' said Jeremy James. 'And it's got a bell *and* a saddlebag.'

'So I see,' said the man. 'An' it's a nice solid job an' all, 'cause I felt 'ow solid it is. When a solid job like that bumps into somebody, the somebody can feel 'ow solid it is.'

The man in the brown overcoat sat down on a garden wall, and pulled a half-smoked cigarette out of his pocket. Jeremy James noticed that the man was wearing grey gloves which his fingers poked out of, and on the man's feet were some black shoes that his toes poked out of.

'Aren't your fingers and toes cold?' he asked the man.

'Don't know,' said the man. 'Can't feel 'em.'

'Well you should have asked Santa Claus to give you shoes and gloves for Christmas,' said Jeremy James. 'Only you're too late now.'

'Santa Claus never brings me nothin' anyway,' said the man. ' 'E don't 'ave time for people like me.'

'Do you mean you didn't get *any* Christmas presents?' said Jeremy James. 'Not even from your Mummy and Daddy?'

'That would 'ave bin a surprise,' said the man. 'They've bin dead twenty years. No, sonny, nobody gives presents to ole blokes like me. People either walk straight past you, or they knock you down.'

'I didn't *mean* to knock you down,' said Jeremy James. 'And I did say sorry.'

'I know that, son,' said the man. 'An' *you* stopped to talk to me, didn't you?'

The man puffed his cigarette, and blew a little cloud of smoke into the air. He really was a very dirty man – his hair, his face, his clothes and even his fingernails were dirty.

'Why are you so dirty?' asked Jeremy James.

'Protection,' said the man. 'Dirt protects you against the cold, you see. Now if Santa Claus was to give me a nice warm house an' nice clean clothes, an' a nice warm Christmas dinner, I wouldn't need all this dirt.'

'I don't think Santa Claus gives that sort of present,' said Jeremy James. 'I think you have to do work to get that.'

'I expect you're right,' said the man. 'And that's why I'm so dirty.'

All the same, Jeremy James thought it a bit unfair that the man in the brown overcoat should have had no Christmas present at all, and a plan began to form in his mind. It was a plan that needed to be thought about a little, because after all 50p was 50p, but the thinking didn't last very long.

'Can you wait here for a minute?' asked Jeremy James.

'Well, I expect so,' said the man. 'I don't 'ave any urgent appointments for today.'

'Brrm brrm!' said Jeremy James, and pedalled at world record speed away from the man in the brown overcoat. 'I'll be back in a minute!' he called as he pedalled.

And back in a minute he was. With a loud 'Errgh!' he screeched to a halt right beside the man in the brown overcoat. Then Jeremy James got off his tricycle, and went to his saddlebag.

'Now close your eyes and hold out your hand,' he said to the man in the brown overcoat.

The man did as he was told, and when he opened his eyes again, he found that his hand was holding a completely full packet of liquorice allsorts.

'It's a Christmas present,' said Jeremy James.

223

The man in the brown overcoat looked at the packet of liquorice allsorts, then he looked at Jeremy James. Then he looked at the packet again, and then again at Jeremy James.

'What's your name, son?' he said at last.

'Jeremy James,' said Jeremy James.

'Well, Jeremy James,' said the man, 'it's the best Christmas present I've ever 'ad. An' if Jesus 'isself was to give me a present, it couldn't be better'n this one. I'll remember you, Jeremy James.'

Then the man in the brown overcoat stood up, and patted Jeremy James gently on the head with a half-gloved hand.

'I must be on me way now. But I'll always remember you, Jeremy James.'

'Merry Christmas, then,' said Jeremy James.

'Merry Christmas to you, too,' said the man.

And the man walked slowly away in one direction, while Jeremy James brrm-brrmed at top speed in the other. There was, thought Jeremy James to himself, a great deal to be said for having Christmas every day.

How the Lion Lost His Lunch

For my father,
and in loving memory of my mother

Contents

CHAPTER ONE

Going Away

Mummy had spent the morning cooking, cleaning the house, dressing Christopher and Jennifer, and packing suitcases. Daddy had spent the morning putting the roof rack on the car. It was a very difficult roof rack to put on, as Daddy kept explaining to Mummy when he came in for a breather, for a screwdriver, or for sticking plaster. It was one of those roof racks which had a mind of its own. If one side was straight, the other was crooked, and if Daddy straightened out the crooked side, then the other side would go crooked. And when both sides were finally straight, the clamps got themselves hidden. And when Mummy found the clamps, it was the screws that got hidden . . . It really was a difficult roof rack to put on.

Jeremy James tried to help Daddy at first, by holding things for him. Daddy had said, 'We'll soon have this job done,' and Jeremy James had stood there holding things for hours and hours, until eventually Mummy had said he should go and play, while Daddy fixed the roof rack on his own.

All these activities were in preparation for the holiday. There had been an unusual spell of summer sunshine – two days in succession – and the weather forecast had promised more. Mummy had said she could do with a break, and Jeremy James said he could do with a break as well, and as Daddy had nothing urgent to think about doing, they decided to spend a week at the seaside. The day was in fact rather grey and cloudy, but Daddy said it was bound to clear up soon. That was just before he said he'd get the roof rack on soon. But even after the roof rack was on, the day was still grey and cloudy.

'Don't you think you'd better cover the cases?' said Mummy.

'Oh no, it'll brighten up soon,' said Daddy. 'That's what the weather forecast said.'

'Hmmph,' said Mummy. 'I still think you should cover the cases.'

And so Daddy covered the cases. It took him quite a while to cover the cases, and it took quite a while for Mummy to finish sticking bits of plaster on Daddy, but at last the car was loaded and they were all set to leave.

'Have you done a wee?' Mummy asked Jeremy James.

'No, I don't feel like it,' said Jeremy James.

'Go upstairs and do one all the same,' said Mummy.

Jeremy James went upstairs, didn't do a wee, and came downstairs again.

'There's a good boy,' said Mummy.

'Hmmph,' said Jeremy James.

Then they all went out to the car. Christopher and Jennifer were comfortably bedded down in their pram-top at the back, Jeremy James was strapped into his seat, Mummy sat next to Jeremy James so that she could reach the twins, and Daddy was alone at the front. With a whirr, a cough and a roar the engine started first time, and away they went.

'It's started to rain,' said Mummy.

'So it has,' said Daddy. 'Good job I covered the cases.'

It seemed strange to be leaving the house behind. Jeremy James looked back. The windows were closed, the doors were locked, and the upstairs curtains were drawn, as if somehow the house had gone to sleep. Jeremy James waved.

'Who are you waving to?' asked Mummy.

'The house,' said Jeremy James. 'It'll be lonely without us.'

They were soon driving through the town, and Jeremy James enjoyed looking out of the window at the cars, shops and people. Everything was very wet now, because it was raining quite heavily, but inside the car it was warm and dry, which somehow made the journey even more exciting. Jeremy James wondered if all the people outside had realized that this particular car was going on a special journey. He tried to see their faces, and in fact quite a few people did seem to look at the car as it passed by. One or two even pointed, and Jeremy James felt very pleased that they had noticed the particular car going on its special journey.

'We are important,' said Jeremy James. 'People are looking at us.'

At that very moment there was a loud flapping noise, and something fell down over the window, shutting out all the people who had been looking at the important car.

'Oh Lord,' said Daddy, 'it's the tarpaulin.'

The car squealed to a halt, and despite some angry hoots from behind, Daddy jumped out into the pouring rain. Then the car shook and rocked and trembled as Daddy fought with the tarpaulin. Judging by the way Daddy kept rushing round the car, the tarpaulin seemed to be winning, but after a while some raincoated chests and stomachs pressed up against the windows on either side. A voice shouted, 'Have you got it?' and another voice shouted, 'We're all right this side!' and then more voices joined in and more chests and stomachs shut out the rain and the light. Then the car stopped shaking, and the door opened. With cries of 'Thanks very much!' and 'Cheerio!' and 'Do the same for you one day!' Daddy dropped, or rather dripped, into his seat and closed the door.

'Phew,' he said. 'Blooming cases are all soaked through.'

'And so are you,' said Mummy. 'Here, dry yourself with this.'

She passed Daddy a nappy from the back of the car. Daddy looked at it closely.

'Hasn't been used, has it?' he asked.

Mummy laughed and shook her head, and Daddy rubbed his hair and face with the nappy.

'There we are,' he said, handing it back. 'Dry as a baby's bottom. Let's hope I shan't get nappy rash all over my face.'

There were more hoots from behind, and when Jeremy James looked through the rear window, he could see a whole line of cars and buses and lorries. In fact the man in the car behind was just getting out when Daddy said, 'Away we go!' and away they went, squirting a jet of water right up into the face of the man, who shook his fist in the air.

'No patience, some people,' said Daddy, as they cruised through the High Street. 'Remarkably traffic-free for this time of day.'

'I think they're all behind us, dear,' said Mummy. 'That's why they were hooting.'

The rain was coming down even heavier now, and the windscreen wipers clicked out a jolly rhythm as they swished across the glass.

'I thought you said it was going to clear up soon,' said Mummy.

'*I* didn't say it,' said Daddy. 'The weather men said it. They promised fine weather for today.'

'Do you know the men in charge of the weather?' asked Jeremy James, gazing with new admiration at the back of Daddy's head.

'No,' said Daddy.

'Oh,' said Jeremy James, not quite so admiringly.

'And they don't know me,' said Daddy. 'And what's more, they don't know the weather either.'

But in spite of the rain, Jeremy James found it very exciting to be going on holiday, and when they drove on to the motorway, the adventure became even more thrilling. Everyone was racing along, and even Daddy's car managed to overtake some lorries, as well as an occasional car (usually driven by an old lady). Jeremy James pretended that it was a motor race, and every time they overtook someone, it brought them one place nearer the front. He didn't count the times that people overtook them, because those people were in a different race which he called the lunatics' race, as Daddy said they were all lunatics. The real race was between Daddy's car and everything else in the slow and middle lanes. Sometimes there would be a slow car in the middle lane (a slow car was one that went slower than Daddy's), and Daddy would call the driver a middle-lane-hugger who shouldn't be allowed on the motorway. Once, when they passed a middle-lane-hugger, Jeremy James looked back at the driver's face, and he saw the man's lips move to form a word which might just possibly have been 'lunatic'.

'These people shouldn't be allowed on the motorway,' said Daddy. Then he pulled over to leave the way clear for a big black car which had been following them with its headlights flashing.

'Lunatic!' said Daddy as the big black car raced by.

Perhaps it was the excitement, or perhaps it was the influence of the rain streaming down from the sky, or perhaps it was simply the delayed effect of the orange juice at breakfast – but whatever the cause, Jeremy James suddenly became aware of a feeling. It was a feeling that would not go away. And it was a feeling that soon became very strong and very urgent.

'I want to do a wee,' said Jeremy James.

The announcement was not greeted with any enthusiasm from Mummy or from Daddy. Mummy merely said, 'Oh!' and Daddy used his lunatic or middle-lane-hugger voice to inquire: 'Can't you wait?'

'No,' said Jeremy James, 'it's coming.'

'You'd better pull over to the side,' said Mummy. 'Let him do it on the verge.'

'You're not supposed to stop,' said Daddy. 'Except in an emergency.'

Jeremy James wriggled in his seat.

'It *is* an emergency,' said Mummy.

Daddy pulled over on to the hard shoulder, and Mummy unstrapped Jeremy James. She quickly put a raincoat on him, and Daddy got out of the car and came round to open Jeremy James's door. They just got to the grass verge in time.

They were about to walk back to the car, when there was a flashing of lights and a squealing of brakes, and there beside them was a real live police car. Out of the police car came two real live policemen, who stood in front of Jeremy James and Daddy as if they had just stepped out of the television screen.

'What's the trouble, sir?' asked the taller of the two policemen.

'Waterworks,' said Daddy.

'In the engine, sir?' asked the policeman.

'In my little boy,' said Daddy.

'Oh!' said the policeman. 'You know you're not supposed to stop on the motorway, don't you, sir?'

'Yes, I realize that,' said Daddy. 'But it was an emergency.'

236

'You ought to have driven to the nearest exit,' said the policeman.

'My little boy couldn't wait,' said Daddy.

The tall policeman looked very serious, and Jeremy James began to feel rather worried. He knew you weren't supposed to steal, or to kill people, but perhaps there was also a special law that you mustn't wee-wee on motorways. He gazed up at the tall policeman.

'You're not going to put us in prison, are you?' he asked.

The tall policeman looked down at Jeremy James, and then he looked across at the other policeman, who had a round red face that was suddenly covered by a wide grin. The tall policeman crouched down so that he wasn't quite so far away from Jeremy James.

'Do you think we should?' he asked.

'Oh no,' said Jeremy James. 'I didn't know you weren't allowed to wee on motorways.'

'You're not allowed to *stop* on motorways,' said the policeman.

'Oh,' said Jeremy James, 'but I don't think I could wee without stopping.'

The other policeman laughed out loud, and the tall one stood up and patted Jeremy James on the head.

'On your way then,' he said. 'And try not to let it happen again.'

'Have a good holiday,' said the second policeman. 'Hope the weather clears up for you.'

Daddy looked up at the sky. 'You wouldn't think so,' he said, 'but according to the weather men, the sun's shining now.'

'I expect it is, sir,' said the second policeman. 'Just behind those black clouds.'

Mummy strapped Jeremy James into his seat again, and as they drove off, Jeremy James turned and waved to the two policemen. They waved back, and climbed into their car beneath the flashing light.

'Well, that was nice,' said Jeremy James, feeling very pleased with himself.

'Delightful,' said Daddy, as they rejoined the lunatics and the middle-lane-huggers. 'The perfect start to a holiday.'

'And all thanks to me,' said Jeremy James.

CHAPTER TWO

Mrs Gullick

At first Warkin-on-Sea looked exactly the same as the town at home. The roads were the same, the houses were the same, the shops were the same, and the people were the same. And when Daddy stalled the engine at the traffic lights ('Something wrong with the worple worple,' said Daddy), Jeremy James was sure it was the same man hooting from behind who had hooted at them in the rain at home. But when Daddy drove down to the sea front, Jeremy James felt a lot happier. Because the sea front was completely different from any place Jeremy James had ever seen. On one side there were open-fronted shops, cafés, and yum-yummy ice cream parlours. On the other there were stretches of green, with flowers, and benches, and shelters. And beyond that was a wall which wasn't very high, and beyond the not very high wall was ... the sea. Jeremy James could see it even from where he was – miles and miles of moving grey water, stretching as far as the eye could reach. There was enough water there for twenty million baths. If only it was lemonade, thought Jeremy James.

'Can I go in the sea?' he asked.

'Tomorrow,' said Mummy. 'It's getting late now – we must find a hotel.'

'Will we get ice creams as well?' asked Jeremy James.

'You'll have ice creams as well,' said Mummy.

'Oh look!' shouted Jeremy James. 'There's trampolines. Oh and swings . . . it's a playground . . .'

'You'll go to the playground too,' said Mummy.

'And there's a boating lake!' cried Jeremy James.

'Tomorrow,' said Mummy. 'You'll have plenty of time tomorrow.'

'Oh, can't I go today?' asked Jeremy James.

'We must find a hotel first,' said Mummy. 'Then if there's time after that, you can go.'

It was the old grown-up story: first you must do what you don't want to do, and then if there's time you can do what you do want to do.

'Can't we go to the playground first?' he asked, but he knew they couldn't. Grown-ups never change, and Mummy was sure to say no.

'No,' said Mummy.

'I knew you'd say that,' said Jeremy James.

Finding a hotel proved to be a lot harder than expected. Daddy drove along the front, but all the hotels had notices up saying 'no vacancies', which apparently meant they were full. Jeremy James spotted a huge hotel on a hill and said he'd like to stay there, but Daddy said that was the Grand Metropolitan and had five stars, which must have meant that that was full as well. By the time Daddy had driven along the different side roads, round the squares, up the hills and down the dales, it looked as if they would have to go home even before Jeremy James had had a single ice cream, swing, bathe or boat.

They were on their way down towards the seafront for the third or fourth time when Daddy pointed towards an old house set back from the road behind some tall hedges.

'Might be worth a try,' he said. 'Come on, Jeremy James.'

Daddy and Jeremy James got out of the car, and Daddy opened the front gate. Behind the hedges was a large, overgrown garden, and completely hidden from the road was a notice which Daddy read out. It said:

GULLICK HOUSE
Bed and Breakfast
Proprietor Mrs M Gullick
VACANCIES

'Not "no vacancies"?' asked Jeremy James.

'Vacancies,' said Daddy. 'No "no". And no "no" means "yes". Let's go and see Mrs Gullick.'

They walked up the cracked concrete path to the flaking grey front door, and Daddy rang the bell.

Nothing happened for quite a long time, and

Daddy was just raising his hand to ring again when the door opened, and there stood a tall woman with grey hair and a very serious face.

'Yes?' she said.

'Mrs Gullick?' asked Daddy.

'Yes,' said Mrs Gullick.

'Ah,' said Daddy. 'Do you have a room suitable for me and my family? Apart from us, there's my wife and twin babies.'

'Babies,' said Mrs Gullick. 'I haven't got cots. I can't take babies.'

'We've got things they can sleep in,' said Daddy quickly. 'All we need is the room.'

'I've got a room for three,' said Mrs Gullick. 'But nothing for babies.'

'We'll take it,' said Daddy. 'A room for three'll be fine.'

'How long are you staying?' asked Mrs Gullick.

'Just one night,' said Daddy.

Jeremy James tugged at Daddy's coat. 'Not just one night, Daddy,' he said. 'We're staying for a whole week.'

Daddy looked at Jeremy James in the same way as he looked at roof racks and middle-lane-huggers, and then he turned to Mrs Gullick again. 'Um ... ah ...' he said, 'we're ... um ... travelling around, you see. Just one night in Warkin.'

'Then when can I go on the trampolines and things?' asked Jeremy James.

'You'll have plenty of time for that,' said Daddy, in a Mummy-like that's-enough voice.

'I don't see how,' grumbled Jeremy James.

'Just one night, Mrs Gullick,' said Daddy.

'It'll be forty pounds,' said Mrs Gullick. 'And no breakfast for the babies.'

'Phew!' said Daddy.

'I don't usually have babies,' said Mrs Gullick.

'I'm not surprised,' said Daddy.

'And I like to be paid in advance,' said Mrs Gullick.

Daddy pulled out his wallet, and gave Mrs Gullick forty pounds. Then for the first time Mrs Gullick smiled. Jeremy James had never seen a smile quite like Mrs Gullick's smile. It wasn't jolly. It wasn't even friendly. It was simply a widening of the mouth across the surface of the face, more like a drawing of a smile than a real smile. And then she patted Jeremy James on the head, and it felt just like being patted with a dead fish.

'And what's your name?' she asked.

'Jeremy James,' said Jeremy James.

'You'll be a good boy, won't you?' said Mrs Gullick. 'Hm? You won't go putting dirty finger marks on the walls, will you?'

'No,' said Jeremy James.

'Or jumping on the furniture, or stamping on the floor.' She looked across at Daddy. 'We like to keep the house nice and quiet, you see,' she said.

'We'll be as quiet as we can,' said Daddy.

'That's right,' said Mrs Gullick. 'No shouting or screaming, hm, Jeremy James?'

'Well,' said Jeremy James, 'I might shout just a bit.'

'No, no,' said Mrs Gullick. 'If you're not a good boy, I shan't give you any breakfast.'

Jeremy James was about to point out that she *had* to give him breakfast because Daddy had *paid* for it, but Daddy took his hand and he found himself walking back towards the car.

'I don't like her,' said Jeremy James. 'She's creepy.'

'And that,' said Daddy, 'is why we're only staying here for one night.'

A few minutes later, the creepy Mrs Gullick was leading the family up three flights of steep, creepy stairs. The house was dark and musty, and the carpets were faded and worn. On each floor there were gloomy cupboards and tables, and vases without flowers, and on the walls there were old photographs in dull wooden frames. It was the sort of house that would have dead bodies in the cellar and ghosts in the attic. Jeremy James shuddered and took a quick look behind to make sure no one was following him up the stairs.

The room they were to sleep in *was* the attic. It contained a huge brown cupboard with a creaky door, a double bed with brass rails, a small bed with no rails, a dressing table with a cracked mirror, an armchair with a spring poking out of the seat, and a lot of little pictures round the walls – mainly photographs of old men and women.

'You'll be on your own up here,' said Mrs Gullick. 'The bathroom's along the corridor. Only a bath'll cost you extra.'

'What time's breakfast?' asked Daddy.

'Eight-thirty,' said Mrs Gullick.

'Till when?' asked Daddy.

'Just eight-thirty,' said Mrs Gullick.

'Ugh, that's a bit early,' said Daddy.

'It's the normal time,' said Mrs Gullick.

'Could I have some boiled water, please, Mrs Gullick?' asked Mummy.

'Sorry,' said Mrs Gullick. 'I only do breakfasts.'

'It's for the babies' feed,' said Mummy.

'Oh,' said Mrs Gullick. 'Boiled water. Well . . . I don't take babies, you see . . .'

'If you could just fill these two flasks for us,' said Mummy, in her do-as-you're-told voice.

Mrs Gullick went down the stairs, mumbling and muttering.

'What an awful woman,' said Mummy. 'And what an awful place.'

'We'll find a better place tomorrow,' said Daddy. 'But this is the only one with vacancies.'

'I'd be surprised if it didn't have vacancies,' said Mummy.

*

Daddy and Jeremy James went to unload the car, while Mummy saw to the twins, both of whom were now wailing for their supper. When Daddy and Jeremy James had gone down and up the stairs for the third time, they found Mrs Gullick in the room.

'I don't usually have babies,' she was saying. 'They make a noise. I'm not used to them.'

'Haven't you any children of your own, Mrs Gullick?' asked Mummy.

'No,' said Mrs Gullick. 'I don't like children.'

This was too much for Jeremy James. He stood right in front of Mrs Gullick, looked straight up into her long, lined face, and said:

'If you don't like children, then children won't like you, so there!'

There was a stunned silence. Even Mummy and Daddy were too surprised to say anything, and Mrs Gullick stood quite still and expressionless, like a vase without flowers. And then a very strange thing happened. Her face sort of crumpled, and her eyes grew moist, and she began to cry. It was silent crying, a bit like Mummy when she was peeling onions, but Jeremy James could clearly see two large teardrops trickling down the side of Mrs Gullick's nose.

'I'm sorry, Mrs Gullick,' said Daddy. 'He didn't mean it . . .'

'I did mean it,' said Jeremy James, rather more subdued. 'Only I didn't mean it so that you should cry.'

'You're quite right,' said Mrs Gullick. 'I must

seem a rather nasty old woman to you.'

'Yes, you do,' said Jeremy James, a little surprised at Mrs Gullick's knowledge of his thoughts.

'Jeremy James, sh!' whispered Mummy.

'The truth is,' said Mrs Gullick, 'I did once have a little boy of my own. Only I lost him, you see.'

'Oh dear,' said Jeremy James. 'Couldn't you find him again?'

'No,' said Mrs Gullick, very softly. 'No, I never found him again. So it always makes me sad to see children.'

'Well, you should have had some more like Mummy did,' said Jeremy James.

Mrs Gullick put her hand on Jeremy James's shoulder, and as she looked down at him, her face seemed somehow kinder and gentler.

'I couldn't,' she said. 'You see, I lost my husband, too.'

'Oh,' said Jeremy James. 'You must be very careless, losing them both.'

Mummy came to Jeremy James's side.

'I think you've chattered enough now, Jeremy James,' she said. 'Why don't you help Daddy finish the unloading?'

'Come on, Jeremy James,' said Daddy. 'Let's get back to work.'

As they left the room, though, Jeremy James heard Mrs Gullick say to Mummy: 'What a lovely boy. You must be very proud of him.'

And when Mummy said yes, she was, Mrs Gullick

said: 'My son's name was James too. And I'd have been proud if he'd been like your son.'

'You know,' said Jeremy James, as he and Daddy went out of the front door, 'I think Mrs Gullick's quite nice really. In fact, I think I like her after all.'

'Glad to hear it,' said Daddy. 'And I think she likes you, too.'

CHAPTER THREE

Kerdoing

It was bedtime. The family had been to a restaurant in town for their supper, and faced with a limitless choice Jeremy James had chosen the most luxurious dish in the world: fish and chips. He had followed that up with strawberries and cream, and had accompanied the whole meal with a glass of cool Coca Cola. Now he felt very full and rather sleepy.

The twins had been lively all evening, but after a lot of rocking and coaxing they had quietened down. Daddy was in his pyjamas and Mummy was in her nightdress, and Jeremy James had been tucked up in his bed. He felt really cosy. There was something warm and tingly about sleeping in the same room as Mummy, Daddy and the twins – as if they'd got a little world all to themselves.

Daddy stood by the door with his hand on the light switch, and Mummy climbed into bed.

'Kerdoing!' said the bed.

'Oh dear,' said Mummy. 'It's one of those.'

The bed gave another creak and groan as Mummy made herself comfortable. Then Daddy switched off the light, and Jeremy James heard him pad across the room.

'Kerdingadongadoing!' said the bed, and then it creaked and cracked and kerdoinged as if it was on the verge of falling to pieces.

'Oh Lord,' said Daddy. 'Can you move over a bit, love?'

'If I move over any more,' said Mummy, 'I'll fall out of the window.'

'Well, I'm right on the edge here,' said Daddy.

'And I'm right on the edge here,' said Mummy. 'This bed has only got edges.'

There was more loud crunching and squeaking as Daddy heaved himself out of the bed and across the room to the light switch.

Jeremy James sat up to get a good view of the remarkable bed.

'You certainly are on the edge,' said Daddy to Mummy. 'You must have moved.'

'I haven't moved,' said Mummy. 'It's what my mother used to call an M-bed.'

'An M-bed?' said Daddy.

'It sags in the middle,' said Mummy.

'Can I try it?' asked Jeremy James.

'Be our guest,' said Daddy.

Jeremy James climbed into the bed, which said kerdoing to him, too, and although he thought he was on the edge, he found himself nestling up against Mummy.

'It's a bit like a slide,' said Jeremy James.

'More like a retired trampoline,' said Daddy.
'Now what are we going to do?'

'I'll sleep here,' said Jeremy James. 'It's fun.'

'It might be fun for you,' said Daddy, 'but where
are *we* going to sleep?'

'You could sleep on the floor,' said Jeremy James.

'Thanks very much,' said Daddy.

'That's not a bad idea,' said Mummy. 'We could
shift the bed over to the window, and put the mattress
down here on the floor.'

'I see what you mean,' said Daddy. 'That's if the
floor doesn't sag as well. Good idea, Jeremy James.'

Mummy and Jeremy James got out of the bed
and helped Daddy to push it towards the window. It
was a very heavy bed, and they could only move it

an inch at a time, and with every movement it went bump, hump, creak and groan. The noise must have woken Christopher, because he suddenly let out a piercing howl.

'Oh dear,' said Mummy, and stopped pushing the bed so that she could pick Christopher up. 'Jeremy James,' she said, 'could you just sit in the chair and hold Christopher, while Daddy and I finish moving the bed?'

Jeremy James sat down in the armchair, which also said kerdoing, and Mummy carefully placed Christopher in his arms. 'Wah, wah!' said Christopher, kerdoing said the armchair, and bump-hump-creak-groan said the bed, as Mummy and Daddy continued pushing it towards the window.

In the middle of all this loud activity, there was a knock at the door.

'Was that the door?' said Daddy.

'No,' said Jeremy James, 'I think it was somebody knocking at the door.'

Daddy went to the door and opened it. And there in the doorway stood a man in a red dressing gown. The man had a bald head and a twiddly moustache, and an angry expression in between.

'What the devil do you think you're up to?' said the man. 'We can't get any sleep at all.'

'Nor can we,' said Daddy. 'I'm terribly sorry, but we're trying to arrange things so that we *can* get some sleep.'

'Arrange things?' said the man. 'Sounds as if

254

you're moving house! All that banging and crashing.'

'Well, we're shifting the bed so that we can put the mattress down on the floor,' said Daddy. 'The bed sags in the middle, you see, and . . .'

'Oh,' said the man with the twiddly moustache, 'now that's a good idea. Our bed sags as well.'

'It was Jeremy James who thought of it,' said Daddy.

'Clever lad,' said the man. 'I've fallen out of bed twice already. Here, let me give you a hand with that thing.'

And so saying, the man came into the room and helped Mummy and Daddy push the bed across to the window. It still went with a bump and a groan, but it went a lot quicker.

'There, that should do it,' said the man. 'Weigh a ton, these old beds. Pity they didn't make the middle as solid as the ends, eh?'

'Thanks very much for your help,' said Daddy. 'Can I come and do the same for you?'

'That's all right, I'll manage. Damn good idea that. We've been here three days and I haven't had a wink. Good night to you.'

And off he went. Daddy relieved Jeremy James of Christopher, who was quiet now, and Mummy got the bed ready on the floor.

'Fancy sticking this for three days!' said Daddy. 'No wonder Mrs Gullick likes to be paid in advance.'

When the bed was ready, and Christopher was back in the pram-top, and Jeremy James was snug and cosy, and Mummy was curled up on the mattress, Daddy turned out the light.

'Ah, that's better!' said Daddy, as he slid between the covers with no creaks except from his knees. 'Peace and quiet at last.'

And just then there was a loud bumping and humping from down below.

'Ah,' said Daddy, 'that'll be the moustache following our example.'

'I expect everyone'll be shifting beds soon,' said Mummy. 'Maybe by breakfast time, we shall all be asleep.'

A loud voice came from down below: 'Will you stop that infernal noise! There's people trying to sleep!'

And then Jeremy James heard the voice of the man with the twiddly moustache: 'Awfully sorry. We're shifting the bed so we can put the mattress on the floor.'

'Mattress on the floor?' said the first voice.

'So we can get some sleep!' said the twiddly moustache.

'I say,' said the first voice. 'That's a good idea.'

'Little boy upstairs thought of it,' said the twiddly moustache.

After that there was a good deal more banging and creaking from down below, and Jeremy James heard more voices, though they weren't so distinct. But by now he was so tired that he couldn't really be bothered to listen to what they were saying. The last thing he heard was Mummy and Daddy laughing from the floor, and the last thing he thought was what fun it was to be on holiday. And then he went off into a lovely deep sleep.

CHAPTER FOUR

The Lost Ones

It was very early in the morning when Jeremy James crept down the dark, creaky stairs of Mrs Gullick's house. Up in the attic, Mummy and Daddy were fast asleep, phwee-phewing and grrr-hoik-rumbling from their mattress on the floor, while the twins lay quietly in their pram-top. Jeremy James had been awake for hours, and he had been thinking about Mrs Gullick and her lost husband and son. He knew from experience that losing things can be a very upsetting business. He was always losing sweets and bits of chocolate. Mummy said he lost them down in his tummy, but even if you lost things in your tummy, it still meant you hadn't got them any more.

Once Mummy and Daddy had thought they'd lost Jeremy James. They'd gone out for the evening, and Jeremy James had played hide-and-seek with the babysitter. He'd been so good at hiding, while the babysitter was so bad at seeking, that the babysitter had sent for the police. Of course, Jeremy James hadn't been lost at all, because he knew just where he was. Fast asleep in Daddy's tool shed. But Mummy and Daddy had *thought* he was lost, and they'd certainly been unhappy. So it must be much worse for Mrs Gullick, because not even Jeremy James knew where her husband and son were. And so Jeremy James had decided to try and find them, and that was why he was creeping down Mrs Gullick's stairs.

At the foot of the stairs was a door, and although it seemed unlikely that Mr Gullick and James would hide in such an obvious place, Jeremy James opened the door just to make sure.

'What the devil . . .?' said a vaguely familiar voice.

Jeremy James looked around, looked up, and then looked down, and there on the floor was a shiny head and a twiddly moustache poking out from under a blanket.

'Oh it's you,' said the man. 'You've come to the wrong room, sonny.'

Next to the shiny head and twiddly moustache was a head that was covered with curlers and an expression of wide-eyed surprise. Jeremy James decided that neither of these heads belonged to the Gullicks, and he quickly closed the door.

'In any case,' said Jeremy James to himself, 'Mrs Gullick would have looked in all the doors you can see. It's no good looking in doors you can see. I'll have to find a door you can't see.'

Jeremy James walked slowly along the passage, ignoring all the doors he could see, and looking hard for a door which he couldn't see. But he didn't see

one. The only interesting thing he did see was a pair of shoes standing in front of one of the ordinary seeable doors. They were nice shoes, black and shiny, and whoever had lost them would obviously be very upset at losing them. Jeremy James decided that it would be helpful if he could place the shoes where the person might find them most easily. He thought hard for a moment.

'The only place where everybody has to go,' said Jeremy James to himself, 'is the front door. So if I put them outside the front door, the man is sure to find them.'

Jeremy James picked up the shoes and carried them all the way down to the ground floor. Then he walked along the passage to the front door, opened it, and put the shoes on the step outside.

'He can't miss them there,' said Jeremy James. 'And I'll bet he'll be pleased to find them.'

When Jeremy James closed the front door and turned round, he suddenly noticed a curtain in the hall. It was a dark curtain that covered the back of the stairs, and if it hadn't been for a shaft of sunlight falling on it, he probably wouldn't have noticed it at all.

'I wonder,' said Jeremy James, 'I just wonder if . . . perhaps . . . there might just possibly . . .'

Slowly he pulled the bottom of the curtain to one side. And behind the curtain, completely hidden from sight, was a door. Even Mrs Gullick could never have spotted that door behind the curtain. It was the sort of door you would only see if you were looking for a door that *nobody* could see.

'That's where they are,' said Jeremy James. 'No wonder Mrs Gullick couldn't find them.'

He pulled the curtain again to reveal the door handle, reached up, and turned it. The door didn't open. He tugged hard. The door yielded a little, but something seemed to be holding it closed.

'Maybe Mr Gullick is pulling it the other way,' thought Jeremy James. 'Because he doesn't want to be found.'

Jeremy James took a deep breath, puffed out his chest like a pigeon, and gave the door an almighty heave. It flew open, and Jeremy James lost his grip and fell hard on his bottom. When he picked himself up, he found himself confronted not by Mr Gullick, but by a flight of stone steps that led downwards into very uninviting, very ghostly, very dead-body darkness. Jeremy James stood on the top step and peered down.

'Mr Gullick,' he called softly. 'I can see you!'

But Mr Gullick remained unseen.

'I've found you!' said Jeremy James.

But Mr Gullick remained unfound.

Then Jeremy James noticed a light switch on the wall by the door. Perhaps Mr Gullick had switched it off so that he wouldn't be seen. Jeremy James smiled, and switched it on.

'I'm coming,' he said. 'Here I come, Mr Gullick.'

Slowly and carefully he eased his way down the steep stone steps, holding tightly to the rail at the side. At the bottom he found himself in a huge, gloomy room lit only by a single bulb, which seemed to throw more shadows than it did light. Jeremy James stood quite still, until his eyes had grown accustomed to the gloom, and then he started to go forward in order to investigate all the interesting objects that lay scattered over the floor. But at that very moment there was a loud *crash* at the top of the steps, and Jeremy James was so startled that his body almost jumped off his legs.

When Jeremy James had put himself together again, he looked up, and to his horror he saw that the door was tightly closed. He scrambled up the steps as fast as he could, turned the handle, and

pushed. But the door wouldn't open. He banged on it with his fists, he kicked it, he bumped it with his bottom, he charged it with his shoulder, he shouted 'Help!' at the top of his voice . . . but still the door remained tightly closed. Maybe this was what had happened to Mr Gullick and James: they had hidden down here, the door had gone crash, and they'd never been found again.

Jeremy James sat on the top step. His eyes were stinging, and the sting soon changed itself into tears that went rolling down his cheeks and plopping on to the second step. Mummy and Daddy would wake up and see that he wasn't in his bed. They'd hunt in all the cupboards and all the boxes and all the beds. They'd hunt in the bathroom, the bedrooms, the garden, the tool shed. But nobody would ever dream of pulling aside the dark curtain behind the stairs. Not even the police would think of that. And after a while, Mummy and Daddy would load the twins into the car and drive slowly and sadly away from Warkin-on-Sea, and they'd tell everybody they'd been to the seaside and lost Jeremy James. The thought was too terrible to think, and the tears plopped faster and faster on to the second step.

But heroes don't get out of difficult situations by sitting on steps and crying. And so after a while Jeremy James wiped his eyes on his pyjama sleeve, tightened up his lips, and asked himself: What would Daddy do? Well, Daddy would think about it, and then . . . he'd ask Mummy what to do. So what would Mummy do? Mummy would say: 'Don't be silly, of course you can open the door.'

So Jeremy James banged, kicked, bumped, charged and shouted again. But the door wouldn't open.

'I can't,' he said. 'It won't move.'

So now what would Mummy do? She'd probably say: 'Let's have a cup of tea.' Only that was no good either. What had Mummy said the other day when those silly jigsaw pieces had refused to go in? 'If they won't go in one way, try them another way.' And they *had* gone in, too. 'If you can't go out one way,' Mummy would say, 'try another way.'

Jeremy James went down the steps with a determined look on his face. There must be another door or a window somewhere. He walked slowly all round the walls. No doors, no windows. He looked up at the ceiling. No doors or windows there either. He looked at the floor. Nothing but piles of boxes and . . . was that a rocking horse? Jeremy James went nearer. Yes, it was. Rather different from his rocking horse at home, this one was big and clumsy and covered with dust, but . . . Jeremy James got on and, yes, it rocked very well, even though it squeaked and groaned rather like the kerdoinging bed. And what was that over there? Jeremy James dismounted, and inspected the next object. It was a pram – a very old pram with dusty hood and rusty wheels.

'That's James Gullick's pram,' said Jeremy James,

'and James Gullick's rocking horse. I wonder why he keeps them down here?'

Next to the pram was an old cot, and in the cot was a teddy bear with one ear. It wasn't a soft cuddly teddy bear, but was hard and patchy.

'Your toys are a bit funny,' said Jeremy James. 'My Mummy and Daddy give me much nicer things to play with.'

Jeremy James looked inside some of the boxes, and they were also full of old things – lampshades, books, newspapers, clothes, paintings. One nice wooden box looked as if it might contain a treasure, but when Jeremy James opened it, all he found was some bundles of letters tied up in ribbons. Some of the boxes had cobwebs on them, and when a big spider danced across Jeremy James's finger, he decided the boxes were not worth looking into anyway. And he started getting nasty tickly feelings all down his spine and over his face.

'I wish I could find a way out of here,' he said, and his eyes began to sting again.

Meanwhile, there was a great deal of activity in the house. Mummy was trying to cope with a pair of hungry twins, Daddy was knocking on people's doors and asking whether anyone had seen Jeremy James, the man with the twiddly moustache was trying to fix up his bed, which had collapsed last night when he had moved it across to the window, and a short man with a monocle and a grey suit was walking barefoot up and down the passage looking for his shoes. The man with the twiddly moustache told Daddy about Jeremy James's visit, but the man with the monocle hadn't seen any little boys, and in any case he wasn't interested in little boys, he was interested in his shoes. Daddy and the man with the twiddly moustache walked up and down shouting 'Jeremy James!' and the man with the monocle walked down and up shouting 'Where are my shoes?' and some other people poked their heads out of their doors and shouted 'What's the matter?'

A short time before, Mrs Gullick had collected her newspaper from the front door, noticed that the cellar door was open, and so closed it. Now she left off preparing the breakfasts in order to investigate the disturbance.

'What,' said Mrs Gullick, 'is the meaning of this shouting?'

'Ah, Mrs Gullick,' said Daddy. 'You haven't seen Jeremy James, have you?'

'No, I haven't,' said Mrs Gullick.

'Ah, Mrs Gullick,' said a voice further up the stairs. 'You haven't seen my shoes, have you?'

'No,' said Mrs Gullick, 'I haven't.'

'Did you clean them?' said the voice, which was soon followed by the man with the monocle.

'No,' said Mrs Gullick, 'I didn't.'

267

'But I left them outside my door,' said the man with the monocle.

'Then outside your door,' said Mrs Gullick, 'is where they should be.'

'Well they're not,' said the man with the monocle.

'Then they must be somewhere else,' said Mrs Gullick.

'Mrs Gullick,' said Daddy, 'are you sure you haven't seen Jeremy James?'

'No, I haven't,' said Mrs Gullick. 'Wasn't he with you last night?'

'Of course he was,' said Daddy. 'But when we woke up this morning, he was gone.'

'So were my shoes,' said the man with the monocle.

'Perhaps,' said the man with the twiddly moustache, 'your Jeremy James has walked off with this gentleman's shoes.'

'My Jeremy James,' said Daddy, 'would never walk off anywhere without having his breakfast. Could he have got himself locked in anywhere, Mrs Gullick?'

A thought came into Mrs Gullick's head. She had wondered at the time, but had assumed that the wind had blown the door open.

'Just a moment,' she said.

Daddy, the man with the twiddly moustache, and the barefooted man with the monocle followed Mrs Gullick along the hall to the back of the stairs.

Mrs Gullick pulled aside the curtain, and tugged open the cellar door.

'Jeremy James, are you down there?' she called.

'Yes I am, yes I am!' came the voice of Jeremy James. 'Don't close the door!' And he came racing up the stone steps, out of the door, and into Daddy's arms.

'What on earth were you doing down there?' asked Daddy, lifting him up high and holding him very tight.

'I was looking for Mr Gullick and James,' said Jeremy James.

'Oh, good heavens!' said Mrs Gullick. 'But they're both dead, Jeremy James.'

'Dead?' said Jeremy James. 'But you said you'd lost them.'

'Lost,' said Daddy, 'is just a way people have of saying that someone is dead. I'm ever so sorry, Mrs Gullick.'

Mrs Gullick dabbed her eyes. 'What a dear, sweet boy,' she said, and hurried off to the breakfast room to have a little cry.

'I suppose,' said the man with the monocle, 'your little boy doesn't happen to have seen my shoes, does he?'

'You haven't seen a pair of shoes wandering around, have you, Jeremy James?' asked Daddy.

'Black shoes?' asked Jeremy James. 'Shiny black shoes?'

'That's right,' said the man with the monocle. 'I left them outside my bedroom door.'

'Oh, I thought they were lost,' said Jeremy James. 'Or rather, dead. I put them outside the front door so you'd find them.'

The man with the monocle went to the front door, opened it, and stepped gingerly outside.

'Come on, Jeremy James,' said Daddy. 'I think Mummy's waiting for us upstairs.'

He winked at the man with the twiddly moustache, and they set off up the stairs at top speed, with Jeremy James jogging up and down on Daddy's shoulder.

'This is much better than James's old rocking horse,' said Jeremy James.

'I don't know about James's old rocking horse,' said Daddy. 'But it's certainly better than a shiny black shoe on your bottom.'

CHAPTER FIVE

Castles in the Sand

Jeremy James was sorry to leave Mrs Gullick's, and Mrs Gullick was sorry to say goodbye to Jeremy James. But she gave him a large bar of chocolate 'for the journey', and this helped greatly to sweeten the parting.

When they were out of sight from Mrs Gullick's, Daddy set off to look for another hotel, while Mummy and Jeremy James pushed the twins' pram in the direction of the beach. On the way they stopped to buy a bucket and spade, and Jeremy James put the spade over his shoulder and oompah-oompahed down to the golden sands of Warkin-on-Sea. And as his feet sank into the soft carpet, it was like stepping into another world. The first men to step on the moon couldn't have been more excited than Jeremy James stepping on to the beach at Warkin-on-Sea. Mummy spread a large blanket over the sand and then helped Jeremy James into his bathing costume, and he gazed wide-eyed all round him. There were lots of people on the beach: all ages and

272

colours and shapes and sizes. Near by lay a man with
a huge tummy.

'Oh Mummy,' said Jeremy James, 'do you think
he's got twins in his tummy?'

'Sh!' said Mummy. 'Don't talk so loud! Of course
he hasn't. Men don't have babies.'

'But isn't he fat!' cried Jeremy James.

'Sh, Jeremy James!' said Mummy. 'He'll hear
you.'

'No he won't,' said Jeremy James. 'He's asleep.'

At that moment the fat man waved away a fly
that had mistaken his stomach for a giant slide.

'Anyway,' whispered Jeremy James, 'I expect he
knows he's fat. He'd have to be silly not to know
he's fat.'

'Yes, all right, Jeremy James,' said Mummy, 'just don't shout about it.'

'Where's the sea gone, Mummy?' asked Jeremy James.

'It's gone out,' said Mummy. 'It's what's called low tide. It goes out and then comes in again.'

'You mean like Daddy when he's doing the gardening?' asked Jeremy James.

'Something like that,' said Mummy with a smile.

'What are those red flags for out there?' asked Jeremy James.

'They're to warn people not to go any further,' said Mummy. 'Nobody must go beyond those flags.'

'Why, Mummy?' asked Jeremy James.

'Because it's dangerous,' said Mummy.

'Why is it dangerous?' asked Jeremy James.

'Because you can get caught by the tide,' said Mummy.

'How can you get caught by the tide?' asked Jeremy James, but Mummy had had enough of the questions, and shooed Jeremy James off to go and build sandcastles while she stretched out on the blanket with the twins.

Jeremy James wandered off with his bucket and spade until he found a good spot that nobody had dug up, pressed down, or sat on. And here he set out to break the world record for brilliant sandcastle building. He began to dig a large, circular moat, and although the circle gradually became less and less round and more and more square with sudden diversions, Jeremy James felt he was doing well. And then suddenly a familiar voice said:

'That's not a very good moat.'

Jeremy James looked up from his digging, and there stood a ginger-haired, freckle-faced boy with a very superior expression on his face. His name was Timothy Smyth-Fortescue, and he lived in the big house next door to Jeremy James's. Timothy Smyth-Fortescue had everything, did everything, and knew everything.

'It's all over the place,' said Timothy. 'Moats should be round, not all over the place.'

'I'll bet you couldn't dig a better one,' said Jeremy James.

'Oh yes I could,' said Timothy. 'That's my castle over there, and it's miles better than yours.'

'I've only just started mine,' said Jeremy James.

'Well, your moat's all crooked,' said Timothy. 'Moats should be round, not crooked.'

'I didn't want a round moat,' said Jeremy James. 'I wanted mine to be crooked.'

'Why?' asked Timothy.

'Because,' said Jeremy James.

'Because what?' asked Timothy.

'Because . . .' said Jeremy James, 'because round moats are old-fashioned. My Daddy told me round moats are old-fashioned. People don't build round moats any more.'

'You're just saying that,' said Timothy, 'because

you can't build a round moat. You don't know how to.'

'Oh yes I do,' said Jeremy James.

'Go on then,' said Timothy. 'Make a round moat.'

'I won't,' said Jeremy James.

'You can't,' said Timothy. 'You come and look at my castle, and then you'll see how proper castles are built.'

'Right,' said Jeremy James, with a determined look on his face. 'You show me your rotten castle. I'll bet it's a rotten castle. I'll bet your castle isn't nearly as good as my castle's going to be. 'Cos I'm going to build the best castle *anybody's ever* built.'

By now they had reached Timothy's castle. And it wasn't a rotten castle at all. It was a very good castle. In fact it was so good that it may well have been the best castle anybody had ever built. It had a completely round moat, lots of smooth regular towers, battlements, a drawbridge. It looked just like a real castle.

'There you are,' said Timothy. '*That's* how to build a sandcastle. And I'll bet *you* couldn't build a sandcastle like that.'

'It's all right,' said Jeremy James. 'But I've seen better ones.'

'Where?' demanded Timothy.

'Places,' said Jeremy James.

'What places?' demanded Timothy.

'Well,' said Jeremy James, 'places like . . . like . . . the Grandmother Polly Ann . . .'

'The what?' said Timothy.

'The Grandmother Polly Ann. It's a hotel . . .'

'You mean the Grand Metropolitan,' said Timothy. 'That's where I'm staying. And I haven't seen you there.'

'No,' said Jeremy James, 'because I'm not staying there, because we didn't want to stay there. *We've* been at Mrs Gullick's, so there.'

'The Grand Metropolitan's got five stars. I'll bet Mrs Gullick hasn't got five stars,' said Timothy.

'Who cares about stars?' said Jeremy James. '*I* had two eggs and two slices of bacon for breakfast.'

'I had poached haddock,' said Timothy. 'And four slices of toast.'

'Mrs Gullick gave me a big bar of chocolate, too,' said Jeremy James.

'Chocolate's bad for your teeth,' said Timothy. 'You shouldn't eat chocolate.'

'And you shouldn't eat poach taddock,' said Jeremy James. 'Poach taddock makes people die.'

'No it doesn't,' said Timothy.

'Yes it does,' said Jeremy James. 'I know somebody who died of poach taddock.'

'Who?' asked Timothy.

'My Mummy's Great-Aunt Maud. She ate poach taddock, and they had to put her in a box and throw her away.'

The conversation would doubtless have continued, but at this moment Timothy's mother, in a swimming costume and sunglasses, approached the sandcastle.

'Come along, Timothy,' she said, 'we're going back to the hotel now. Oh hello, Jeremy. Fancy seeing you here! Have you come with your mummy and daddy?'

'Yes, Mrs Smyth-Forseasick,' said Jeremy James, who always had some difficulty with Timothy's mother's name.

'Well, say hello to them for me, Jeremy,' said Mrs Smyth-Fortescue.

Jeremy James was about to remind her that his name was Jeremy *James* when she suddenly said something that he found very interesting indeed.

'What a beautiful sandcastle!' she said. 'That *is* good! Did you build that all by yourself, Jeremy?'

'No,' said Jeremy James, 'I didn't build it at all. Timothy built it.'

'Timothy,' said Mrs Smyth-Fortescue, 'did you tell Jeremy that *you* built it?'

Timothy's face went red, and he looked down at his right foot which was burying itself as deep as possible in the sand.

'You mustn't say things like that, dear,' said Mrs Smyth-Fortescue. 'It's very naughty to tell lies. Come along now, perhaps you can play with Jeremy again this afternoon. Say goodbye, dear.'

'G'bye,' said Timothy, still studying his right foot.

'G'bye,' said Jeremy James. 'Hope you have poach taddock for lunch.'

Off went Timothy with his mother, and Jeremy James returned to his crooked moat. Perhaps his sandcastle wouldn't be quite the best anybody had ever built, but at least it would be his. Jeremy James gave a cheerful smile, and began to dig.

CHAPTER SIX

The Donkey

Jeremy James had swung and trampolined, he had boated and merry-gone-round, and now he was all set for a donkey ride over the sands. There were twelve donkeys in all, and when Jeremy James and Daddy arrived, eleven of them already had riders. The twelfth had stuck his nose in a bucket of hay and was munching as happily as if it were a bucket of strawberries and cream. Daddy lifted Jeremy James up into the saddle, and gave some money to a young man who wore swimming trunks and a straw hat.

'Off we go then!' said Straw Hat. 'Come on, Speedy!' And he gave Jeremy James's donkey a slap.

Off went the young man, and off went eleven donkeys, but Jeremy James's donkey kept his feet in the sand and his nose in the bucket.

'He's not moving,' said Jeremy James.

Daddy gave Speedy a slap and cried: 'Off we go!' But off Speedy did not go.

'Oy!' shouted Daddy after the young man with the straw hat, but the young man simply strolled

on, followed by eleven plodding donkeys with eleven contented riders. And the twelfth donkey munched his hay.

'I don't think he wants to go,' said Jeremy James.

'We've paid for a ride,' said Daddy, 'and a ride is what you shall have.'

Daddy pulled hard on the bridle, and went very red in the face, but Speedy didn't move.

'Having trouble?' asked a fat man with a wobbly tummy.

'Donkey won't go,' said Daddy. 'We paid our money, and he refuses to move.'

'I'll give you a hand,' said the fat man.

Then Daddy pulled and the fat man pushed. They pulled and pushed till they were both puffing like steam engines, but Speedy stood as still as a rock.

'He doesn't want to go,' Jeremy James told the fat man. 'That's the trouble.'

'Don't keep saying that!' said Daddy. 'He's *got* to go. One more effort!'

Daddy pulled and the fat man pushed, and the donkey took one step forward and trod on Daddy's foot.

'Ow!' said Daddy, and let go of the bridle.

'Oof!' said the fat man, and fell on his tummy.

'Hee haw!' said Speedy, and returned to his bucket of hay.

'It's no good,' said the fat man, getting up from the sand. 'You'll have to wait till the owner comes back.'

'Looks like it,' said Daddy, sitting down in the sand and holding on to his foot. 'He just doesn't want to go, that's the trouble.'

Daddy waggled his foot, and the fat man wobbled away, and Jeremy James sat on Speedy wondering how he could persuade the donkey to move. Daddy had tried ordering, coaxing, pushing and pulling, but Daddy was never very good at getting things to go. Jeremy James remembered the car, the washing machine, the TV set, and even his railway set refusing to go when Daddy told them to. Daddy asking Speedy to move was just like Jeremy James asking Mummy for ice cream instead of potatoes – a waste of breath and time.

'If I was a donkey,' said Jeremy James to himself,

'I'd certainly stay still when Daddy told me to go. And that's a fact.'

But the donkey also stayed still when Jeremy James told him to go. And this gave Jeremy James an idea. If the donkey stayed still when he was told to go, what would he do if you told him to stand still?

Jeremy James leaned forward in the saddle, and whispered in Speedy's ear: 'Stay here, Speedy. Good boy. You stay here.'

Speedy raised his head from the bucket, gave a wheezy sort of grunt, and slowly trotted away.

Daddy scrambled to his one good foot. 'Hey, come back!' he shouted.

This seemed a little strange to Jeremy James, as Daddy had just spent such a long time trying to get Speedy to move off. But it didn't matter anyway, because Speedy simply trotted a little faster.

'Go back!' cried Jeremy James, and Speedy went forward, as Daddy came limp-hobble-puffing after them.

Jeremy James looked down, and the sand became a golden blur beneath Speedy's pounding hooves. But they had to go faster still if they were not to be caught by the thousand Red Indians that were chasing them.

'Slow down!' shouted Jeremy James. 'Speedy, slow down!'

'Oh dear!' said a pretty girl in a red bathing costume. 'Look at that little boy. He wants the donkey to slow down, and it's going even faster!'

'I'll stop them!' said the young man who was sitting next to the pretty girl. 'You watch me!' And he stuck out his chest and ran in front of Speedy, waving his arms and shouting: 'Whoa!'

'Let him catch you,' whispered Jeremy James, and Speedy promptly swerved right round the young man, who lunged, missed, and fell flat on his face.

'Come back!' cried the young man, on his knees in the sand.

'Come back!' cried Daddy, falling even further behind.

'Go back!' cried Jeremy James, with a smile all over his face.

And Speedy sped on. Two boys playing football leapt out of his path, and a lady with a Pekinese dog said 'Good heavens!' as donkey and rider raced by. 'Wuff wuff!' said the Pekinese dog, and chased after Speedy. 'Come back, Montague!' shouted the lady, and chased after the Pekinese dog.

The sight of all these running figures attracted the attention of a brown dog and a black dog, and before long there was a trail of dogs, dog-owners, men, women and children, and – last of all – Daddy chasing Speedy and Jeremy James along the beach.

'Slow down!' cried Jeremy James, thoroughly enjoying himself, and Speedy ran faster and faster.

No doubt they would have ridden right off the sand, out of Warkin-on-Sea and as far as the Rocky Mountains if the young man with the straw hat had not caught hold of Speedy's bridle.

'Whoa there, Speedy!' he cried, and to Jeremy James's disappointment, Speedy came to an abrupt halt. So too did the Pekinese dog, four other dogs, five dog-owners, six children, seven men and women, and – eventually – Daddy.

'I dunno what you been up to,' said Straw Hat. 'Gallopin' like a racehorse he was!'

'I haven't been up to anything,' said Jeremy James. 'He wouldn't go.'

'Wouldn't go?' said Straw Hat. 'Wouldn't go! He'd have won the Derby goin' like that!'

'It's not the boy's fault!' said a man with a black dog and a red face. 'You should keep your donkeys under control.'

'Hear, hear!' said the woman with the Pekinese. And 'Wuff wuff!' said the Pekinese.

'Are you all right, Jeremy James?' asked Daddy, panting through the crowd.

'Yes thank you,' said Jeremy James.

'He's a little hero,' said a woman. 'The way he stayed on that donkey! I'd have been terrified!'

Then several people in the crowd murmured: 'Hero... very brave... could have been a disaster...'

Jeremy James smiled heroically as Daddy lifted him off the saddle and on to his shoulders.

'That donkey,' said Daddy to Straw Hat, 'is very dangerous. He nearly broke my foot, and he could easily have injured my son.'

People in the crowd mumbled: 'Dangerous...

could have been killed . . . should be prosecuted . . . licence taken away . . .' and other long words that sounded threatening. Straw Hat looked very uncomfortable. Finally, he dipped his hand in the leather bag that hung from his shoulder, and pulled out a handful of coins.

'Sorry, mister,' he said. 'Perhaps you could buy your lad an ice cream to make up for it.'

Jeremy James smiled even more heroically.

'Can't understand it, though,' said Straw Hat. 'Speedy never bolted before. We call him "Speedy" as a joke, 'cos he's always so slow.'

The crowd dispersed, and Jeremy James rode Daddy back along the beach. It was a slow, bumpy ride, not nearly as exciting as the gallop on Speedy. But when Jeremy James realized that it was in fact a limp towards the ice cream van, he began to enjoy the return journey almost as much as the first ride.

It was while he was unwrapping his Moon Rocket Lolly that Jeremy James happened to glance back up the beach again. There in the distance he could see the young man in the straw hat, and the young man was pulling hard at the bridle of a donkey that was obviously refusing to move.

'Looks like Speedy's got stuck again,' said Daddy.

'That,' said Jeremy James, 'is because Straw Hat's not saying the right thing to him.'

'Aha!' said Daddy. 'And what *is* the right thing?'

'The right thing,' said Jeremy James, licking his Moon Rocket, 'is the wrong thing.'

Daddy smiled. 'Well, I must remember that,' he said.

But Jeremy James knew Daddy didn't really understand. Grown-ups are often very slow when it comes to understanding children. And donkeys.

CHAPTER SEVEN

Totty Botty

The new hotel had no creaking beds, no dark stair-
cases, no mysterious cellars. It was very clean, very
modern, and rather boring. It had a posh restaurant,
though, and Jeremy James decided that it was time
he varied his diet. He therefore chose chicken and
chips, followed by strawberries and ice cream, and
accompanied by Coca Cola.

'I thought you were going to try something different,' said Daddy.

'I am,' said Jeremy James. 'I'm having chicken.'

'He usually has fish,' said Mummy.

The waiter, who had black hair, a black moustache and a black jacket, bent low over the table.

'Would sir lika da tomato ketchuppa widda
chips?' he asked.

'Pardon?' said Jeremy James.

'Would you like tomato ketchup?' said Daddy.

'Oh, yes please,' said Jeremy James.

'Tell the waiter, then,' said Daddy.

The waiter was writing something down on a
pad.

'Yes, please,' said Jeremy James, but the waiter didn't seem to hear. Instead he finished writing, and then bent low again.

'Anda da lemon inna da Coca Cola, ha?'

'Why doesn't he talk properly, Daddy?' asked Jeremy James.

'He's asking if you want lemon in your Coca Cola,' said Daddy.

Jeremy James looked straight up at the waiter. 'You talk funny,' he said. The waiter looked straight down at Jeremy James. 'I no talka funny,' he said. 'You hear funny.'

Mummy and Daddy both laughed, and so did the waiter, but Jeremy James frowned.

'He's Italian,' whispered Mummy, when the waiter had gone. 'He doesn't come from this country. That's why he doesn't speak English properly.'

'Why doesn't anybody teach him?' whispered Jeremy James.

'I expect they've tried,' whispered Mummy. 'But English is a very difficult language.'

'Is it?' whispered Jeremy James. 'I don't think it is. I speak properly, and I'm not nearly as old as he is.'

'Ah, but do you speak Italian?' asked Daddy.

'What's Italian?' asked Jeremy James.

'Hm,' said Daddy, 'how do you explain that?'

'Different people,' said Mummy, 'come from different countries, and so they speak different languages. Like we say "eat" and the French say

291

"manger" and the Germans say . . . what do the Germans say?'

' "Essen",' said Daddy. 'And the Italians say "mangiare". Different people have different words.'

'Well that's silly,' said Jeremy James. 'Why don't they have the same words? Then they wouldn't have to talk in a funny way.'

'You're right,' said Daddy. 'It would make life easier if everyone spoke the same language. But which language should everybody speak?'

'English,' said Jeremy James.

'But that,' said Daddy, 'would only make life easier for *us*.'

At that moment, an elderly man who was sitting at the next table leaned across and grinned at Daddy.

'*Voilà l'Anglais typique!*' he said, pointing at Jeremy James.

Daddy laughed and said something else that Jeremy James couldn't understand, and then he and the other man started making all kinds of strange noises with their noses and throats.

'That's French,' whispered Mummy. 'Daddy and the man are speaking French.'

But the more Jeremy James listened, the less like speaking it seemed. The elderly man made his noises very fast, and sounded as if he was holding his nose, and Daddy occasionally made some noises of his own, though these were slower, and Jeremy James recognized one sound that he knew, which was "er". But even Daddy wasn't using proper words, and although he and the elderly man laughed as if they understood each other, Jeremy James knew that this must be some silly game.

All through the meal Jeremy James was unusually quiet. When Mummy asked him if his chicken was all right, he simply grunted, and when Daddy asked him if he was full, he merely nodded. And when the waiter said: 'Issa good, no?' he looked up and said 'Mhm, mhm!'

It was only when they were back in the hotel bedroom (where the twins were already asleep) that Jeremy James began to talk in words again. Mummy said to him:

'Bedtime now, so get your pyjamas on.'

And Jeremy James said: 'Cobbly wobbly chucka-bung bung.'

'Pardon?' said Mummy.

'Wobble wabble doople dums,' said Jeremy James. 'And socky dock.'

'Good heavens!' said Daddy. 'Our son's speaking a foreign language!'

'Dabble gabble,' said Jeremy James. 'Umbly totty botty.'

'Aha,' said Mummy, 'now I wonder what language it is.'

'It's certainly not English,' said Daddy. 'And it doesn't look as if he understands English either. Do you understand English, Jeremy James?'

'Totty botty,' said Jeremy James.

'Totty botty,' said Daddy. 'No, I don't recognize

that language at all. Listen, Jeremy James, if you understand me, nod your head. And if you don't, then shake your head.'

Jeremy James shook his head.

'Aha,' said Daddy, 'caught you there. If you didn't understand, how did you know you should shake your head?'

'Soppy loppy maddy Daddy,' said Jeremy James.

'And totty botty to you,' said Daddy.

'If he doesn't get himself undressed for bed,' said Mummy, 'I shall give him a smack on his totty botty.'

Daddy knelt down in front of Jeremy James and looked at him very seriously.

'Clothes,' said Daddy, waving his arms, 'offy toffy. Pyjamas, onny ponny. And then ready steady beddy.'

Jeremy James gazed straight back into Daddy's eyes.

'Silly billy,' he said.

'And silly billy to you, too,' said Daddy. 'Now if Jeremy James gets his clothes offy woffy and his pyjamas onny wonny and dives straight into beddy weddy before Daddy counts up to one hundred, Jeremy James will have some more ice creamy dreamy in the morning.'

With a sudden flurry of activity, Jeremy James began to undress at world record undressing speed. Daddy stood up, and winked at Mummy.

'The trouble with you English,' he said, 'is that

you never bother to learn other people's languages. Isn't that right, Jeremy James?'

Jeremy James nodded.

'But I'll tell you one thing, Jeremy James,' said Daddy. 'You'd better learn some English by the morning. Or you won't know what type of ice cream to ask for.'

'Issa good,' said Jeremy James. 'I speaka da English good.'

Mummy let out such a shriek of laughter that it woke Christopher up, and Christopher howled a howl which would have been understood in any language. But he didn't understand at all when Daddy told him to quieten down, and it was only when Mummy had picked him up and rocked him in her arms that he finally got the message.

'He no speaka da English,' said Daddy to Jeremy James.

'He too young,' said Jeremy James. 'Gotta da lot to learn.'

CHAPTER EIGHT

The Castle Treasure

'Are we doing anything special today?' asked Jeremy James.

'We're going to Warkin Castle,' said Mummy, putting an arrow-straight parting in Jeremy James's hair.

'A castle!' said Jeremy James. 'A real castle? With a moat and a drawbridge and dungeons and . . .'

'I expect so,' said Mummy.

'And things to torture people with?' asked Jeremy James.

'Like blunt razor blades,' said Daddy, dabbing his chin with a piece of cotton wool.

'I expect they've got everything there,' said Mummy, 'including sharp spikes for people like Daddy who can't get up in the morning.'

'Well, I had a shocking night,' said Daddy. 'All those car doors slamming. Slept better at Mrs Gullick's.'

'Can we go back to Mrs Gullick's then?' asked Jeremy James.

'No,' said Daddy. 'I like to suffer in comfort.'

Eventually Daddy had finished yawning, rubbing his eyes, and dabbing his chin, and the family set off for Warkin Castle. Jeremy James kept a look-out for horses and knights in armour, but apart from the donkeys on the sand and the padded cricketers in the park, there was nothing much to see in the way of horses or knights.

Nor, as it turned out, was there very much in the way of castles. Warkin Castle had no moat, no drawbridge, no dungeons, no instruments of torture, no battlements, no roof . . . in fact, the harder Jeremy James looked, the less castle he could see. There were a few bits of wall scattered over the top of the hill, and there were piles of stones which looked as if they might be good for climbing, but the rest of Warkin

298

Castle consisted of green grass and blue sky.

'Shall I buy a guidebook?' asked Daddy, as they waited at the ticket office.

'May as well,' said Mummy. 'Then we'll know what we're not seeing.'

'Do we have to pay to go in?' whispered Jeremy James to Mummy.

'Afraid so,' said Mummy.

Jeremy James frowned. This was a terrible waste of good money. Perhaps Mummy and Daddy hadn't realized that there wasn't any castle. Grown-ups often do miss things that children see straight away. More than once Jeremy James had spotted an ice cream van while Mummy and Daddy were looking quite the wrong way, and it was surprising how frequently they failed to notice interesting things like toy shops and cafés and playgrounds.

'Mummy,' he said, tugging at her dress. 'You shouldn't pay. They've taken the castle away.'

But it was too late. Daddy had bought the tickets and the guidebook.

'Jeremy James says we shouldn't have paid,' Mummy told Daddy. 'Because they've taken the castle away.'

Daddy laughed. 'Quite right,' he said. 'It must be run by the government. You always have to pay them for things they take away.'

'Anyway,' Mummy said to Jeremy James, 'it's what's called a ruined castle. There *used* to be a castle here.'

'I don't think you should have to pay for something that *used* to be here,' said Jeremy James. 'I'd sooner pay for an ice cream that *is* here than a castle that isn't.'

They walked across the grass, with the twins bumping up and down in their pram, and Jeremy James looked scornfully round at the bits of wall and piles of stones. Daddy raised his nose from the guidebook and announced that they were now passing through the great gate.

'Doesn't look much like a gate to me,' grumbled Jeremy James. 'It's just a pile of stones.'

'Ah no, wait a minute,' said Daddy. 'My mistake. The great gate was back at the ticket office. Ugh, this is just a pile of stones. Let's see . . .'

Daddy seemed to have some difficulty in reading the guidebook, because every so often he would turn it sideways or backwards or upside-down, wave his arm around, and mumble things like: 'Kitchen . . . over there . . . or is it there . . . worple worple . . . blooming diagram . . .'

He did manage to work out that the castle had been built in the fifteenth century, which made it over five hundred years old, but as Jeremy James said, there wasn't anything clever in being over five hundred years old if you weren't there any more.

The only interesting item Daddy found in the guidebook was the fact that a treasure was supposed to lie buried somewhere in the castle, but it seemed to Jeremy James that as there was no castle left, it was highly unlikely that there would be any treasure left either. However, when Mummy and Daddy sat down on a bench with the twins, he decided he might just as well hunt for treasure as sit looking at grass and sky. At least it would be a good excuse for climbing on the walls.

'Stay where we can see you,' said Mummy. 'And don't go climbing on the walls.'

A look of great pain crossed Jeremy James's face. 'Well, can I just *look* at the walls?' he asked.

'Keep right away from them,' said Mummy. 'Those walls are dangerous.'

As walls didn't move, didn't scratch and didn't bite, Jeremy James asked how they could possibly be dangerous. Daddy pointed to a pile of stones and explained that once that pile had also been a wall, and he wouldn't like Jeremy James to be underneath when a wall decided to change into a pile of stones.

'So keep away from the walls,' he said, 'if *you* don't want to become a buried treasure.'

'But they're bound to have put the treasure in the walls!' said Jeremy James.

'People bury treasure in the ground,' said Daddy, 'If it's not in the ground, it won't be anywhere.'

Jeremy James had once found a treasure buried in the back garden. It hadn't been quite what he'd expected, because when he'd finally managed to break it open with a pickaxe, nothing had come out except a shower of water, and Mummy and Daddy hadn't been very pleased. But it proved that Daddy

was probably right, and the ground *was* where people buried their treasure.

Jeremy James wandered over the hill. His mind went back to Mrs Gullick's secret door behind the curtain. Perhaps on the hill there was a patch of grass that wasn't grass at all, but a curtain hiding a secret door that would lead down into the treasure chamber. Jeremy James kept his eyes firmly fixed on the ground as he walked, and . . .

Bump!

'Where are you going, young man?' asked a crackly voice from high above the waistcoat that Jeremy James had bumped into.

Jeremy James looked up past a white beard and into a pair of twinkling blue eyes.

'Sorry!' said Jeremy James. 'I didn't see you.'

'That's all right,' said the man with the white beard. 'I didn't see you either. Are you enjoying yourself then?'

'No,' said Jeremy James.

'Oh,' said the man with the white beard. 'Why not?'

'Because it's boring,' said Jeremy James. 'Castles should have moats and dungeons and torture things – not just piles of stones.'

'Well, it used to have them,' said the man, 'but then it got old and lost them all. The same thing happens to people.'

'People don't have moats and dungeons,' said Jeremy James.

'That's true,' said the man.

'And I was looking for a treasure,' said Jeremy James, 'but I expect the castle's lost that too.'

'Treasure, eh?' said the man.

'Yes,' said Jeremy James. 'It's supposed to be buried in the ground, but I can't find it.'

'Well, you keep searching,' said the man. 'You have to be patient to find buried treasure. But have a quick look up every now and then, just to see where you're going.'

The man with the white beard smiled, and Jeremy James fixed his eyes on the ground and resumed his search. But the grass and weeds and stones were as empty of treasure as the hill was empty of castle. He was just about to give up and go back to Mummy and Daddy when he heard the crackly voice again.

'I say, young man! Over here! Come and look over here!'

The man with the white beard was standing in some high weeds that came almost up to his knees, and he was waving his arm. Jeremy James ran across to him.

'Now I'm not quite sure,' said the man, 'but I've got a funny feeling that if you look very closely in here, you'll find some treasure. You'll have to look hard, mind.'

Then he chuckled and walked away. Jeremy James bent down and looked very hard amongst the weeds. He stepped forward a pace, then another pace, and . . . just where the man had been standing, wedged under a small stone, was the unmistakable silver glint of a fifty pence piece.

Jeremy James picked it up and rushed back to Mummy and Daddy.

'Look what I found!' he cried. 'It's treasure!'

'Where did you get it?' asked Mummy.

'Over there in the weeds!' said Jeremy James. 'The man with the white beard told me where it was. Look, there he is!'

Jeremy James waved, and in the distance the man with the white beard waved back. Then he disappeared behind a wall.

'There are some nice people around,' said Mummy.

'But I wonder how he knew it was there,' said Jeremy James.

'Perhaps he knows a lot about treasure-hunting,' said Daddy.

'And about treasure-hunters,' said Mummy with a smile.

CHAPTER NINE

The Red Flag

The family were down on the beach. Mummy was in her bathing costume, basking with the twins, and Daddy was gradually shedding his raincoat, jacket, pullover and shirt as the hot sun defied the weather forecasters, who had announced that there would be rain today.

Jeremy James picked up his bucket and spade, and went off to build a castle. This would be a real castle not a ruined castle, and it would be surrounded by a deep round moat that would be deeper and rounder than any moat had ever been before. He carefully selected a stretch of smooth level sand, and began to dig.

'You have to build the castle first,' said a familiar voice. 'You don't dig a moat before you've built the castle. Everyone knows that.'

'You don't know anything about sandcastles,' said Jeremy James.

'Oh yes I do,' said Timothy. 'I've built hundreds of sandcastles.'

306

'You didn't build the sandcastle the other day,' said Jeremy James.

'I've built thousands of better castles than that,' said Timothy.

'Let's see them,' said Jeremy James.

'You can't see them now,' said Timothy. 'They all get squashed by the sea. You don't know anything.'

'Oh yes I do,' said Jeremy James. 'I know lots of things that you don't know.'

'Such as?' said Timothy.

'Such as . . .' said Jeremy James, 'such as . . . I know how old Warkin Castle is.'

'500 years old,' said Timothy. 'I've been there. It's all ruined.'

'You don't know what Italian is,' said Jeremy James.

'Oh yes I do,' said Timothy, 'because I've *been* to Italy. I've heard Italian people speaking Italian, so there.'

'Well, I'll bet you don't know what those red flags along the beach are for,' said Jeremy James.

'They're not for anything,' said Timothy. 'They're just flags.'

'They are for something,' said Jeremy James, 'and you don't know what.'

'They're for decoration,' said Timothy. 'To make the place look cheerful. Everyone knows that.'

'You're wrong,' said Jeremy James, 'and you don't know everything, so there.'

'Well what are they for, then, clever?' asked Timothy.

'They're to stop the tide from catching you,' said Jeremy James.

Timothy's nose, which had been dipping in the direction of his toes, now suddenly rose in the air so that he could look down it again.

'The tide couldn't catch me,' he said. 'I can run faster than the tide. I don't need any old red flags to stop the tide from catching me. Anyway, flags can't stop anything. Flags can't move, can they? That's all silly talk.'

'You mustn't go beyond the flags,' said Jeremy James.

'Course you can,' said Timothy. 'Come on, I'll show you.'

'No, you're not supposed to,' said Jeremy James.

'You're scared,' said Timothy. 'I'll race you there. I bet I can run faster than you.'

'No you can't,' said Jeremy James.

'Yes I can,' said Timothy.

And so the two of them raced over the sand, with their legs whirling and their faces twisted in determination. About halfway there, Jeremy James knew he'd won. Timothy wasn't even in the corner of his eye, and there was no sound of thudding footsteps in pursuit. But Jeremy James simply drove himself harder, and didn't stop until he had reached the red flag. Then puffing and snorting, rather like a sleeping Daddy, he turned to look for Timothy. There was no sign of him.

'That showed him,' said Jeremy James. 'I'm the world champion.'

'I'm over here,' came a voice from somewhere along the beach. 'And I won.'

Jeremy James looked round. Level with him, quite a way along the sand, stood another red flag, and beneath the other red flag stood Timothy, waving his arm and shouting: 'I won! I won!'

'No you didn't!' shouted Jeremy James.

'Yes I did!' shouted Timothy. 'You went to the wrong flag!'

'*You* went to the wrong flag!' shouted Jeremy James. 'And you're a rotten cheat!'

'Come over here,' shouted Timothy. 'I want to show you something.'

Jeremy James didn't feel like going over there. Jeremy James didn't feel like being with Timothy at all. Timothy couldn't possibly show Jeremy James *anything* that Jeremy James would want to see.

'Come on!' shouted Timothy.

'I won't!' shouted Jeremy James.

'All right, don't!' shouted Timothy. 'You'll be sorry! I don't care!'

Jeremy James decided he'd better go and see what it was. He could always run away afterwards.

'Look!' said Timothy, stretching out his foot.

'What?' asked Jeremy James, who couldn't see anything.

309

'My foot,' said Timothy.

'What about your silly foot?' asked Jeremy James.

'It's on the other side of the red flag,' said Timothy. 'And I haven't been caught by the tide, have I?'

Jeremy James looked more closely at the foot. It *was* on the other side of the flag, and a little trickle of water was just passing over it.

'Anyway,' said Jeremy James, 'most of you is on this side of the flag. You won't be caught if you're on this side of the flag.'

'You don't know anything,' said Timothy. 'I could go miles past the flag and the tide still couldn't catch me.'

'My Mummy says it's dangerous.'

'I bet your Mummy doesn't know anything either.

Grown-ups just say things like that to frighten children like you. I could go right out there to the sky, and the tide wouldn't catch me.'

'No you couldn't,' said Jeremy James. 'You'd get lost.'

'How could you get lost in the sea!' sneered Timothy. 'It's just water. There's no streets in the sea.'

'Getting lost,' said Jeremy James, 'is just a way people have of saying getting dead. Don't you know that? You'd be dead, so there.'

Jeremy James felt something cold and wet slither against his foot, and when he looked down, there was water coming over his toes. Even though he was standing on the right side of the flag, he had a funny feeling that the tide could still catch him, and he took a big step backwards.

'You're scared,' said Timothy, and took a big step forwards. 'I'm on the other side now, but I haven't been caught, have I? Look!' He took another step. And then another. There was a loud squelch every time he lifted his foot out of the sticky mud, but Jeremy James had to admit that Timothy seemed very un-caught at the moment.

'Are you coming?' called Timothy. 'Or are you too scared?'

'I'm not scared!' said Jeremy James.

'Come on then!' said Timothy.

The trouble with grown-ups is that sometimes they're right and sometimes they're wrong, but there's no way of knowing which type of sometimes

311

it is. So did the tide catch people, or didn't it? Well, it hadn't caught Timothy. There he was, jumping around a long way from the red flag, and he actually seemed to be enjoying himself. People don't enjoy themselves when they're being caught by the tide, do they? But if Mummy was right, Timothy might stop enjoying himself.

Jeremy James looked round to see if there was a grown-up he could ask. 'Excuse me,' he would say, 'but is it true that the tide catches people if they go past the red flag?' Then the grown-up would either say yes, and Jeremy James would be the world champion know-all, or no, in which case he could go leaping into the water and Timothy couldn't accuse him of being scared.

But there were no grown-ups to ask. Timothy and Jeremy James were completely alone by the red flags.

'You're scared!' shouted Timothy.

Jeremy James frowned. This was a real problem. If you're scared, how do you appear unscared without doing the thing you're scared of? Jeremy James thought hard and then harder. And suddenly his frown cleared, his head rose, and his heart lightened.

'I've just got to go and see about something!' he shouted, and before Timothy could shout back, Jeremy James was racing away from the sea and towards Mummy and Daddy. After all, no one can be accused of being scared when they've got to see about something. Seeing about something is much more important than jumping around in the sea. And there was no way Timothy could know that the something Jeremy James was seeing about was nothing.

Daddy had just taken off his vest, shoes and socks when Jeremy James finished breaking the world record for that particular stretch of beach.

'Hullo, Jeremy James,' said Daddy. 'I was just coming to get you. You've saved me the trouble.'

'Oooh, is it teatime?' asked Jeremy James.

'All he ever thinks about is his stomach,' said Mummy.

'No I don't,' said Jeremy James, 'I think about chocolate and ice creams and strawberries . . .'

'Actually,' said Daddy, 'I was coming to bring you away from those red flags. Didn't Mummy tell you it was dangerous to play round there?'

'Yes,' said Jeremy James, 'but I didn't go past them. Timothy did, but I didn't.'

'Was that Timothy from next door?' asked Daddy.

'Yes,' said Jeremy James. 'Worse luck!'

'Where is he now, then?' asked Daddy.

'He's still out there,' said Jeremy James. 'I told him he'd get caught by the tide, but he didn't believe me.'

'He's in the sea?' said Daddy. 'Are you sure?'

'Yes,' said Jeremy James.

'Come on,' said Daddy. 'You'd better show me where he is.'

Jeremy James started to run down the beach with Daddy, pointing to the flag where Timothy had gone

into the water, and then Daddy rushed away from him as if he'd been fired from a rocket. Jeremy James had never seen Daddy move at such speed. If Daddy had been chased by a bull, he couldn't have run any faster than he was running now. Jeremy James's world record for that particular stretch of beach was totally shattered as Daddy hurtled past the red flag and into the water. Jeremy James watched him splashing and squelching, and the water was up to his ankles, his shins, his knees . . . and still Daddy went on. And then Jeremy James saw and heard what Daddy was splashing towards. Standing in the sea, with water right up to his chest, was Timothy, and he was shouting and crying at the same time.

'Hold on!' called Daddy. 'I'm coming!'

'Help, blubber, blubber, help!' came the sound of Timothy's voice.

Daddy caught hold of him, swept him up in his arms, and carried him back out of the sea. Timothy was twitching like a fish, and his mouth was a bit like a fish's too, opening and shutting and turned right down at both corners.

As Daddy walked back up the beach with Timothy in his arms, and with Jeremy James at his side, Mrs Smyth-Fortescue came running to meet them.

'What happened?' she cried.

'He's all right, Mrs Smyth-Fortescue,' said Daddy, 'he had a bit of a scare, that's all. You're all right now, aren't you, Timothy?'

But Timothy was still too busy shivering and crying to be able to say whether he was all right or not. He clung to Daddy like a limpet to a rock, and Daddy offered to carry him back to the hotel, which Mrs Smyth-Fortescue said was not far away.

'You ought to know,' said Daddy, as the four of them went up the steps and away from the beach, 'that if it hadn't been for Jeremy James, your son might not have lived to tell the tale.'

'What happened, Jeremy?' asked Mrs Smyth-Fortescue.

'Jeremy *James*,' said Jeremy James. 'Well, I told him not to go past the red flags or the tide would catch him, but he didn't believe me. Because he doesn't know very much, you see. So I went and told Daddy that Timothy was in the water.'

'I don't know how to thank you,' Mrs Smyth-Fortescue said. 'You saved Timothy's life.'

By now they had reached the hotel, which was one of those along the front. Mrs Smyth-Fortescue took a pound coin out of her purse and gave it to Jeremy James.

'Thank you!' said Jeremy James, beginning to enjoy life-saving. 'That's my second treasure in two days!'

'Isn't your husband here, Mrs Smyth-Fortescue?' asked Daddy.

'No, he's away on business,' said Mrs Smyth-Fortescue. 'It's just Timothy and me here at the moment.'

'Well,' said Jeremy James, 'I don't think you should let Timothy play on his own again. I might not always be able to save his life.'

At this moment Mrs Smyth-Fortescue was taking Timothy out of Daddy's arms. Timothy raised his tear-lined face and poked his tongue out at Jeremy James. Jeremy James poked out his own tongue and waved the pound coin in the air.

Mrs Smyth-Fortescue thanked Daddy and Jeremy James again, then went into the hotel, carrying Timothy up against her shoulder.

'What was the name of that hotel?' Jeremy James asked Daddy as they walked back to the beach.

'Ocean View,' said Daddy. 'Why?'

'I thought so,' said Jeremy James. 'He wasn't even staying at the Grandmother Polly Ann.'

CHAPTER TEN

Monkeys and Lions

It was the last day of the holiday. Jeremy James looked sadly out of the car window at the sea, the trampolines and the merry-go-round. He could see the donkeys trudging along the beach, led by the young man in the straw hat, and he wondered if Speedy was walking or standing still today. The sun was shining, the sand was golden, the sky was blue, and it was a perfect day not to end a holiday.

'Can't we leave tomorrow instead?' asked Jeremy James.

'Daddy has to work,' said Mummy.

'Who invented work?' asked Jeremy James.

'Nobody invented it,' said Mummy. 'It's just there and has to be done.'

'Well, I wish someone would invent an unwork,' said Jeremy James, 'so that we could stay on holiday.'

But nobody invented an unwork in time to keep Jeremy James at Warkin-on-Sea, and away they went in the direction of what was to be the final treat of the holiday. They were heading for a safari park. Mummy explained to Jeremy James that this was something like a zoo, but instead of people wandering around looking at the animals, the animals wandered around looking at the people. There would be elephants and lions and tigers, and the people sat in their cars while the animals walked free.

The safari park sounded exciting, and when eventually the car drew up at the ticket office, even the twins were happily cooing away like two pigeons on an elephant's back.

The ticket man looked through the window. 'You're not going to feed them to the lions, are you?' he said to Jeremy James.

'Oh no,' said Jeremy James, 'you're not allowed to feed animals in the zoo.'

When the car drove off again, Jeremy James watched out eagerly for lions amid the trees and bushes. But all he saw was a few cows in a field.

'They're not lions!' he said. 'They're cows!'

'Did you know,' said Daddy, 'that cows eat lions?'

'They don't!' said Jeremy James. 'Do they?'

'Yes, they do,' said Daddy. 'Dandelions.'

'Don't tease,' said Mummy. 'We haven't got to the lion reserve yet. Oh look!'

Through the windscreen Jeremy James saw a leopard skin on stilts. It was only when the stilts began to stalk slowly away that Jeremy James realized it was a giraffe. Then he noticed more giraffes, and some zebras too, grazing at the side of the road. One of them actually walked out in front of the car, and Daddy stopped.

'Always stop at a zebra crossing,' he murmured, and Mummy laughed.

When they had seen enough of the giraffes and zebras, they drove on to the next enclosure, where there were rhinos and elephants. Elephants were Jeremy James's favourite animals, but these elephants proved to be rather boring. They did nothing but snuffle up bundles of hay, and the rhinos were no better, because they just munched away at the grass. And so when it became clear that they were not going to push over a tree or charge at each other or sit on a car and do a Number Two, Jeremy James asked Daddy to move to the next field.

'Monkeys!' said Mummy, with a tone of delight.

'Monkeys!' said Jeremy James, with a tone of disgust.

Mummy and Daddy loved monkeys and thought they were very clever, but Jeremy James thought they were just boring. They couldn't do anything that he couldn't do twice as well, and besides they always had nasty sore-looking bottoms. It was bad enough that they were boring, but it was even worse if you had to look at their sore red bottoms.

'Just look at that!' said Daddy.

As there was nothing else to do, Jeremy James followed Daddy's outstretched arm, looked, and looked again. There were about a dozen monkeys climbing all over a red car. In the red car was a little boy who was laughing, a Mummy who was looking frightened, and a Daddy who was looking furious. The Daddy was hooting, and banging on his windscreen, and trying hard to drive on, though he had to keep stopping because of the monkeys on the bonnet. The monkeys were not just climbing over the car, they were actually pulling bits off it. Jeremy James watched with fascination as one monkey got hold of a strip of silvery metal along the side of the car, and pulled it right away. Another was sitting on the wing tugging the car aerial, and others were playing with the bumpers and wing mirrors.

'Lucky people,' thought Jeremy James.

'Poor people,' said Mummy. 'We ought to try and help them.'

Daddy drew up alongside the other car, and

shouted through the closed window: 'We'll get help!'

The Daddy in the other car waved and said 'Thank you!'

Then before the monkeys could even think of jumping on Daddy's car, he had driven away again like a lunatic on the motorway.

'Oh, can't we stay?' said Jeremy James, with a tone of disappointment.

'I thought you didn't like monkeys,' said Mummy.

'I like *those* monkeys,' said Jeremy James. 'I've never seen monkeys eating cars before!'

But grown-ups are never interested in interesting things, and so even the car-eating monkeys had to be left behind as quickly as possible. In fact, Daddy only slowed down when he caught sight of a black-and-white striped land-rover ('Are they pretending to be zebras, Daddy?') which he hooted at until it came driving across. Then both vehicles stopped. Daddy told the driver about the car-eating monkeys, and the zebra-striped land-rover headed back to the monkey field.

Jeremy James watched it go, and when he next looked to the front, they were passing through some heavy iron gates, which the attendant closed as soon as they were clear.

'Lion country,' murmured Daddy. 'This should be interesting.'

And interesting it was, though not quite in the way Daddy meant. The first bit of excitement came when they spotted a whole pride of lions right by the roadside, tearing great chunks of meat to pieces. Daddy stopped the car, and they watched the jaws and the paws and the claws at work, cracking, crunching, scratching and scrunching away. Then it became even more exciting when a huge, shaggy-maned lion came strolling up to the car and looked through the window straight into Jeremy James's eyes.

'Gosh,' said Jeremy James, 'if I opened the window now, I could actually touch him.'

'If you opened the window now,' said Daddy, 'he could actually touch you.'

'Let's move on,' said Mummy. 'I don't like them so close.'

Jeremy James could hardly believe his ears. Surely not even a grown-up could want to go away when there was a lion just outside the window. He could clearly see the yellowish flecks in its eyes, and the blood and slaver on its jaws. No one could possibly have ever been so close to a lion before. Mummy *couldn't* want to go away.

But Mummy did. 'Go on, John,' she said. 'Start the car.'

It was at this moment that lion country became extra exciting. Daddy did try to start the car. And the car gave a wheezy snort, like a lion with indigestion, and remained where it was. Daddy tried again, and again there was a whirr, cough and splutter, followed by silence. The lion wandered round to Mummy's side of the car and peered in at her and

the twins, licking its lips as if about to eat a giant ice cream.

'John!' cried Mummy. 'Get us out of here!'

'I can't,' said Daddy. 'It won't start.'

Some of the other lions began to look with interest at the whirring, coughing, spluttering creature that was sitting right beside them. Two of them got up and wandered across to have a closer look, so that there were now three lions circling Daddy's car.

'Hoot them!' said Mummy. And so Daddy put his hand on the hooter and pressed. The two new lions took no notice at all, but the first lion, who was still gazing hungrily at Mummy and the twins, jumped back and gave an angry roar. Evidently there was nothing in the Lions' Guide to Human Behaviour to indicate the existence of such a strange sound. But although Daddy hooted again, he still wouldn't go away.

'This *is* exciting,' said Jeremy James. 'Do you think we can sleep here, too? With the lions?'

'I'd die of fright,' said Mummy. 'John, what are we going to do?'

At that moment, a car drew up alongside them. It was a red car, and it had a broken aerial and bits of metal sticking out all over. The little boy inside was laughing, and he waved to Jeremy James, who waved back. The Mummy looked worried, and the Daddy was making signals with his arm.

'Are you stuck?' he shouted through the closed window.

'Yes!' Daddy shouted back.

'We'll get help!' shouted the other man.

'Thank you!' shouted Daddy.

The red car drove off, and Mummy gave a sigh of relief.

'Does that mean we shan't be staying?' asked Jeremy James.

'That's right,' said Daddy. 'We're going to be rescued. Save your neighbour from the monkeys, and he'll rescue you from the lions. Old Warkin proverb.'

Sure enough, in just a few minutes' time there were two zebra-striped land-rovers charging to the rescue. One of them chased away the lions, while the driver from the second attached a rope to Daddy's car and then towed it out of the lion enclosure, and into a big yard where there were several cars and some more land-rovers.

'Thank heaven that's over!' said Mummy.

Jeremy James shook his head. 'I don't think I'll ever understand grown-ups!' he said out loud.

'And I shall never understand lion-tamers!' said Mummy.

'And I shall never understand motor cars!' said Daddy.

Daddy and Jeremy James got out of the car, and while Daddy watched a man fiddling with the engine, Jeremy James watched for the lion he hoped would come roaring into the yard. But the only roar

was that of the engine, and the fiddling man straightened up and told Daddy: 'She'll be all right now, sir. Just the old worple worples got a bit overheated.'

Once again the family settled down in the car, and once again Jeremy James gazed sadly out of the window as they left the car-eating monkeys and the man-eating lions further and further behind. Then suddenly they were back on the motorway, amid the same old lunatics and middle-lane-huggers they had raced on the way to Warkin. Jeremy James sank back in his seat and closed his eyes. The next thing he knew was that Mummy was bending over him, shaking him gently and saying: 'We're home, Jeremy

James. We're home.' And when he looked out of the window, there it was – their very own house, just the same as when they'd left it such a long time ago. Jeremy James scrambled out of his seat, jumped out of the car, and rushed to the front door where he waited impatiently for Daddy to come and turn the key.

As he entered the hall, Jeremy James felt almost as if the house put its arms out to greet him.

'I'll bet the house was lonely without us,' he said.

Then he ran upstairs to look at his room, and everything there was warm and welcoming. Even his favourite teddy bear was lying in bed quietly waiting for him. The pictures on the walls were still the same, and the cupboard and chair were the same, too. They were like old friends, and Jeremy James knew they were as pleased to see him as he was to see them.

'Well, Jeremy James,' said Mummy, when they were all sitting round the table eating their supper. 'Did you enjoy your holiday?'

'Yes, thank you,' said Jeremy James. 'But it *is* nice to be home again.'

'Wouldn't you prefer to live at Mrs Gullick's?' asked Mummy.

'No, thank you,' said Jeremy James.

'Or Warkin Castle, or the totty-botty hotel?' asked Daddy. 'Or the safari park?'

'No,' said Jeremy James. 'I liked Mrs Gullick's,

and the hotel. And I liked the safari park. I liked the safari park a lot. I think all those places are very nice. But I think home is really the nicest place of all.'

Look out for

DAVID HENRY WILSON

Causing Chaos with Jeremy James

Jeremy James has lots of talents. He can foil a pair of criminals, act the part of the Virgin Mary and even stop a train with one finger. In fact, he's brilliant at so many things that sorting out his parents' problems should be easy-peasy. But Jeremy James has one tip-top talent: for causing total chaos – as his parents are about to discover!

A second fabulous bind-up of three
ADVENTURES WITH JEREMY JAMES titles:

CAN A SPIDER LEARN TO FLY?
DO GOLDFISH PLAY THE VIOLIN?
PLEASE KEEP OFF THE DINOSAUR

A selected list of titles available from Macmillan Children's Books

The prices shown below are correct at the time of going to press. However, Macmillan Publishers reserves the right to show new retail prices on covers which may differ from those previously advertised.

Terence Blacker

Ms Wiz Magic	0 330 42039 9	£4.99
Ms Wiz Superstar	0 330 43406 3	£4.99
The Crazy World of Ms Wiz	0 330 43136 6	£4.99
The Amazing Adventures of Ms Wiz	0 330 42040 2	£4.99

Alex Gutteridge

Pirate Polly Rules the Waves	0 330 43304 0	£4.99
Witch Wendy Works Her Magic	0 330 43404 7	£4.99
Princess Posy, Knight-in-Training	0 330 43471 3	£4.99

David Henry Wilson

Causing Chaos with Jeremy James	0 330 44175 2	£5.99
Please Keep off the Dinosaur	0 330 34571 0	£3.99

All Pan Macmillan titles can be ordered from our website, www.panmacmillan.com, or from your local bookshop and are also available by post from:

Bookpost, PO Box 29, Douglas, Isle of Man IM99 1BQ
Credit cards accepted. For details:
Telephone: +44(0)1624 677237
Fax: +44(0)1624 670923
Email: bookshop@enterprise.net
www.bookpost.co.uk

Free postage and packing in the United Kingdom